John Perry

The protesting Christian standing before the judgment-seat of Christ to answer for his protest against that parent church which Christ built upon a rock, etc

John Perry

The protesting Christian standing before the judgment-seat of Christ to answer for his protest against that parent church which Christ built upon a rock, etc

ISBN/EAN: 9783741189500

Manufactured in Europe, USA, Canada, Australia, Japa

Cover: Foto ©Andreas Hilbeck / pixelio.de

Manufactured and distributed by brebook publishing software (www.brebook.com)

John Perry

The protesting Christian standing before the judgment-seat of Christ to answer for his protest against that parent church which Christ built upon a rock, etc

PROTESTING CHRISTIAN

JUDGMENT-SEAT OF CHRIST.

INTRODUCTION.

FROM a sincere desire to promote the eternal welfare of every Christian, allow me, dear reader, to lay before you some few reflections upon a subject, which, of all others, is by far the most important — a subject in which every individual amongst us is equally and awfully interested.[1]

It is a *certain* truth, that *you*, with all the rest of mankind, will one day be summoned to stand before the dread tribunal of Jesus Christ, to give to him a strict account both of the faith you have professed, and of the works you have performed.[2] It is a *certain* truth also, that, if it shall then be found that *your* faith has not been *the true faith*, or that your works have not been in accordance therewith, your condemnation to endless misery will be certain and unavoidable.[3]

Of what vital importance, therefore, it is, that you should consider this awful subject well beforehand, by examining closely into the *real reasons* of your religious

---

[1] Matt. xvi, 26, 27; Luke xii, 18, 19, 20; Joel i, 15; ii, 1, 2, 10, 11; 1 Peter iv, 18; Luke x, 42. [2] 2 Cor. v, 10; John xii, 48; Heb. xi, 6; Rom. ii, 6; Matt. xvi, 27; Luke xvi, 2. [3] Rom. ii, 8; Mark xvi, 16; Tit. iii, 10, 11; Rom. xvi, 17, 18; James ii, 14; Matt. xxv, 41, 46.

belief, and how far your practice corresponds with your faith; in order that, if you should discover, after such examination, any cause of apprehension in either of these respects, you may thus be enabled to take such wise and *timely* precautions, as will prevent those dreadful consequences, which otherwise must unavoidably follow.

Now, it is for the purpose of inducing or enabling you to give to the former of these two points of examination, such serious consideration as its importance requires, that I now present you with the following reflections; to which, from a real solicitude for your eternal happiness, I invite your serious and unbiased attention.

THE DAY OF JUDGMENT ARRIVES.

Since, then, it is certain that *you*, one day, will be summoned to appear before the Judgment-seat of Jesus Christ, to give to him, amongst other things, a strict account of the faith you now profess—just imagine to yourself this awful day of account to have already arrived: imagine that you *already* behold the *Son of Man*, attended by his holy angels, *sitting upon the throne of his glory; and all nations standing together before him;*[1] that you behold the *sign of the Son of Man* (the sign of the cross) *appearing in heaven*—that venerable and sacred sign which, in these days, is so generally ridiculed and despised,—that *then all the tribes of the earth mourn;*[2] *weeping and gnashing their teeth;*[3] *and there is great tribulation, such as was not since the beginning of the world to this time.*[4]

JUDGMENT COMMENCES—PREFATORY ADMONITION.

Imagine, moreover, that, amidst all this anguish and distress of nations around you, the terrible moment at length arrives, when *you*, alarmed and trembling, are called upon to give in your individual account,—that

[1] Matthew xxv, 31, 32. [2] Matt. xxiv, 30. [3] Matt. xxv, 30

one of your *Catholic* neighbors is now standing by your
side, and that the JUDGE addresses you in these or the
like words:—

JUDGE.—Hear thou this word which I take up
against thee:[1] I am the Lord:[2] Give ear and tremble.[3]
I am HE that searcheth the reins and hearts;[4] judging
the secrets of men;[5] and my judgment is according to
truth.[6] Wherefore, if thou *hast believed* and observed
ALL THINGS whatsoever I commanded thee, thou shalt
be saved; but if thou hast *not believed* them, thou shalt
be condemned.[7] For I will render unto all men their
dues:[8] to them who have patiently continued in well-
doing, eternal life: but unto them that have been con-
tentious, and have *not obeyed the truth*, indignation and
wrath.[9]

CHAPTER I.

AUTHORITY AND INFALLIBILITY OF THE CHURCH.

1 ESTABLISHED a church on earth: it was entitled,
"THE CHURCH OF THE LIVING GOD; THE PILLAR AND
GROUND OF THE TRUTH."[10] For *upon a rock* I built
it; and promised, saying, "The gates of hell SHALL NOT
prevail against it."[11] Whosoever hath neglected to hear
that church, with *him* will I deal, as with a *heathen man*
and a publican.[12]

This my church, purchased with my own blood,[13] was
dear to me as the apple of mine eye;[14] *holy and without
blemish;*[15] for I gave myself for it, that I might sanctify
it.[16] I appointed pastors to watch over it,[17] and to
teach in it:[18] and, to enable them to fulfil this important

[1] Amos v, 1. [2] Exod. xx, 2. [3] Joel i, 2; ii, 1. [4] Rev. ii, 23.
[5] Rom. ii, 16. [6] Rom. ii, 2. [7] Matt. xxviii, 20; Mark xvi, 16.
[8] Rom. xiii, 7. [9] Rom. ii, 7, 8. [10] 1 Tim. iii, 15. [11] Matt. xvi,
18. [12] Matt. xvii, 17. [13] Acts xx, 28. [14] Eph. v, 25; Zach. ii,
8. [15] Eph. v, 27. [16] Eph. v, 25. [17] John xx, 21; xxi, 15, 16;
Acts xx, 28; Isaiah lxii, 6. [18] Mark xvi, 15; Matt. xxviii, 19.

commission, I promised that the Spirit of Truth should abide with them *for ever*,[1] and guide them into all truth:[2] and I further promised, that *I myself* would be with them *always*—not merely during the lifetime of my apostles, but during all succeeding ages—*even unto the end of the world;*[3] that is to say, that I would always be *with them and their successors* as long as the world should continue. With them, therefore, I *have* been *ever since* I made that gracious promise. On this account and in this sense did I say to them, "He that *heareth you*, HEARETH ME:[4] to wit, he heard me, who was always with them, teaching by their mouth.[5]

Now, therefore, hear thou this word which I take up against thee! Hast *thou* given ear to the teaching of *that church* which I established?—hast thou given ear to *me* teaching by the mouth of its pastors?

A PROTEST ENTERED.

PROTESTING CHRISTIAN.—LORD, *that* church fell into gross errors, and corruptions, and damnable idolatry: and I would not believe its doctrines, but *protested* against them.

THE PROTEST DISALLOWED.

JUDGE.—This word also I take up against thee!—Thou *faithless* servant! am I then as man, that I should lie; or as the son of man, that I should repent? Have I said, and not done it? or have I spoken, and not made it good?[6] I promised concerning my church, saying, "The gates of hell *shall not* prevail against it."[7] But *thou* sayest, "They *have* prevailed against it; for that it hath fallen off from the truth!" Again, I promised concerning its pastors, saying that I would be with them always unto the end of the world;[8] and that the Spirit

[1] John xiv, 16, 17. [2] John xvi, 13. [3] Matthew xxviii, 20. [4] Luke x, 16. [5] 2 Cor. v, 20. [6] Numb. xxiii, 19. [7] Matt. xvi, 18. [8] Matt. xxviii, 20.

of Truth would also abide with them for ever, and guide them into all truth.[1] But *thou* sayest *otherwise*—for that they have fallen off from the truth! And thus thou hast given me the lie, contradicting and blaspheming the word of God.[2]

APPEAL TO SCRIPTURE TO JUSTIFY THE PROTEST.

PROTESTING CHRISTIAN.—Be not angry, O Lord, with thy servant![3] The Holy Scriptures did teach me that *they* were to be my *rule of faith:* for they told me, that "Whatsoever things were written aforetime, were written for our learning;"[4]—that they were written "that I might believe that thou wast the Christ, the Son of God; and that believing, I might have life through thy name;"[5]—they were written "that I might know the certainty of those things wherein I had been instructed."[6]

They further told me, that they were "able to make me wise unto salvation, through the faith which was in thee;" and that they were "profitable for doctrine, for reproof, for correction, for instruction in righteousness: that the man of God may be perfect, thoroughly furnished unto all good works."[7]

And, moreover, thou didst thyself command me to search them, saying, "Search the Scriptures, for in them ye think ye have eternal life; and they are they that testify of me."[8]

Since, then, in compliance with thy command, *I did search the Scriptures,* and found therein all these glorious properties ascribed to them, as showing the purpose for which they were written, how is it just to condemn me now for *protesting* against *every other* authority in matters of faith, save such only as those Scriptures pointed out to me?

[1] John xiv, 16, 17; xvi, 13. [2] Acts xiii, 45; Titus ii, 5. [3] Gen. xviii, 30. [4] Rom. xv, 4. [5] John xx, 31. [6] Luke i, 4. [7] 2 Tim. iii, 15, 16, 17. [8] John v, 39.

8

JUDGE.—This word also I take up against thee
Thou faithless servant! For *such* a protestation I do
not condemn thee: but for protesting, like the unbelieving Jews, against an authority which those Scriptures
did point out to thee—for *that* do I condemn thee!
That the Scriptures did testify of a teaching authority
established by me, and secured by my infallible promises
in *perpetual* truth, but which thou hast rejected, I have
just shown thee from my own words therein recorded:
but now will I condemn thee out of thine *own* mouth.

Thou hast appealed to the Scripture which saith that
"Whatsoever things were written *aforetime*," that is to
say, in the *books of the Old Law*, "were written for
your learning."[1] But what wast thou to learn from
them? *They* could not have been written to teach thee
the *doctrines of the New Law*, because these doctrines
were not preached until long after those Scriptures had
been written. What then wast thou to learn from
them? Why, *the fact* that the ancient prophecies were
fulfilled *in me*. For *they* were written, as also afterwards were *the signs* which I did, "that thou mightest
believe that *I was the Christ*, the Son of God."[2] For
the fulfilment of the prophecies in the Old Scriptures,
and my miracles or *signs* recorded in the New, both
equally testified "that I was *the Christ*, the Son of
God." They were written, then, that *knowing me to be
the Christ*, thou mightest see the strict obligation of *believing me*, whether teaching by my own mouth, or by
the mouth of my church, which I authorized and commissioned to teach unto the end of the world in my
name; and that, so believing, "thou mightest thus have
life *through my name*."

Now, all this was most clearly explained to thee in
that other Scripture to which thou hast also appealed.
That Scripture was addressed to Theophilus, and it told

him, that *it* was written "that he might know the *certainty* of those things wherein he *had been instructed.*"[1] It was not written, then, that thou mightest gather therefrom my individual doctrines; for *in these* thou wast to be instructed beforehand, like Theophilus and the Bereans,[2] by some other teaching authority; and then, like them read the Scriptures only for a further *confirmation* of thy faith thus already received from instruction — by finding therein the credentials of thy instructors.

Thus, then, the Scriptures did not tell thee they were written that thou mightest learn from them the *doctrines* of faith; but rather that these doctrines were to be learned by instruction from some *other* teaching authority.

Thy next appeal, in like manner, pleads against thee. The Scriptures were said to be "able to make thee wise unto salvation, through the faith which was in me."[3] But what Scriptures were there spoken of? Were they not those which Timothy had known "from a child," and therefore the books of the *Old Law* only? And how were these "able to make him wise unto salvation?" It could not be by teaching him the *doctrines of the New Law,* because they did not contain them. How then? Why, *through the faith* which was in me, and which the preceding verse said Timothy had learned — not from the Scriptures — but from that living teaching authority which I had sent forth: "Continue thou in those things which thou hast learned and hast been assured of, knowing OF WHOM *thou hast learned them.*"[4]

Again, all inspired Scripture was said to be "profitable" — observe, it was not said to be *sufficient,* but only "profitable for doctrine, for reproof, for correction, for instruction in righteousness: that *the man of God* (i. e. God's minister) may be perfect, thoroughly furnished" — not unto a complete system of *faith,* but — "unto all

[1] Luke 1, 4. [2] Acts xvii, 11. [3] 2 Timothy iii, 15. [4] 2 Timothy iii, 14.

good works."[1] The Scriptures therefore, only told thee, that they were "profitable" for these purposes. Why hast thou, then, made them speak, as if they had said they were *of themselves sufficient*—as if they had even said they were *necessary;* thereby doing what they themselves complained of, to wit, wresting them unto thine own destruction.[2]

Thus then, in all these, thy appeals to the Scriptures I find *none* to plead for thee—they *all* stand against thee.

PROTESTING CHRISTIAN.—Oh! let not the Lord be angry, and I will speak yet but this once.[3] Peradventure there shall be found in thy *command to search the Scriptures* whereunto I have appealed, a word in favor of thy servant.

THE APPEAL CONDEMNS THE APPELLANT.

JUDGE.—If I shall find but one word of mine to speak *for* thee, I will not condemn thee for that one's sake.

Thou sayest, I *commanded* thee "to search the Scriptures:" rather shouldst thou have said, I *reproached* the Jews for *abusing* the Scriptures. For what thou callest a command to search them was delivered to those unbelieving Jews after this sort: I told them that John bore witness of me; that the works which I did bore witness of me; and that the Father who had sent me, also bore witness of me. (*John, Chapter V. verses* 33, 36, 37.[*])

· 2 Tim. iii, 16, 17. [2]1 Peter iii, 16. [3]Gen. xviii, 32.

* John V.—*v.* 33. Ye sent unto John and he bare witness unto the truth......
v. 36. But I have a greater witness than that of John: for the works which the Father hath given me to finish, the same works that I do, bear witness of me, that the Father hath sent me.
v. 37. And the Father himself which hath sent me, hath borne witness of me. Ye have neither heard his voice at any time, nor seen his shape.

But they would receive none of these testimonies: and for this their unbelief, I reproached them, saying, "whom the Father hath sent, him ye believe not." (*Verse* 38.) I then referred them to the Scriptures of the *Old Law*, which also bore witness of me; for in those Scriptures they trusted, although in truth they did not believe what they taught. (*Verses* 45, 46, 47.) "Search the Scriptures" then, I said, (still reproaching them for their unbelief,) "Search the Scriptures; for in them ye think," —observe I did not say, in them ye *have*, but—"in them ye THINK ye *have* eternal life;" to wit, in thus rejecting me whom the Father hath sent; "and they (Scriptures) are they that testify of me." (*Verse* 39.) "And" though those very Scriptures in which ye trust, thus testify of me, yet "*ye will not come to me, that ye might have life*," through my teaching. (*Verse* 40.) "I am come in my Father's name, and ye receive me not: if *another* shall come in *his own name*, him ye will receive." (*Verse* 43.)

Now, IN ALL THIS, *thou* hast imitated those unbelieving Jews. For, *whom I had sent*, (to wit, the Pastors of my church, commissioned by me to teach in every age unto the end of the world[1]—and for the perpetual

---

[1] John xx, 21; Mark xvi, 15, 16; Matt. xxviii, 19, 20; 2 Tim. i, 13; 2 Timothy ii, 2; 1 Timothy i, *v*. 11, compared with *v*. 18; Tit. i, 5, 9.

v. 38. *Ye have not his word abiding in you: for whom he hath sent, him ye believe not.*

v. 39. *Search the Scriptures, for in them ye THINK ye have eternal life*, and they are they that testify *of me*.

v. 40. And ye *will not come to me*, that ye might have life.

v. 43. I am come in my Father's name, and ye receive me not: if another shall come in his own name, him ye will receive.

v. 45. Do not think that I will accuse you to the Father: *there is one that accuseth you, even Moses, in whom ye trust.*

v. 46. For had ye believed Moses, ye would have believed me: for he wrote of me.

v. 47. But if *ye believe not his writings*, how shall ye believe my words?

truth of whose teaching I had pledged my sure word,[1])
them thou believedst not. Thou searchedst the Scriptures:
they bore witness of this perpetual, unerring, teaching
authority, which I had sent, for they testified of my
plain words, which gave it *commission,*[2]—of my infallible promises, which gave it *security,*[3]—and of my
positive command, which, by obliging all to hear and
obey it, gave it *authority.*[4] But, like the unbelievng
Jews, thou wouldst not in truth believe what the Scriptures thus clearly taught; although, like those Jews,
thou trustedst in them. For, *as they,* searching the
Scriptures of the Old Law, thought they found testimony against *me* and *my* teaching,[5] *so thou* in like manner,
searching the Scriptures of the New Law, fondly per-
suadedst thyself that thou hadst found therein testimony
against the authoritative teaching and perpetual truth
*of that church which I had established to teach in my
name.* For in the Scriptures *thou thoughtest thou hadst*
eternal life, in *protesting* against that perpetual and unerring church; whereas, the Scriptures were they that
testified of it—and although they thus testified of it, yet
thou *wouldst not come to it,* that thou mightest have life
through its teaching; for *its* teaching was *my* teaching:
"He that heareth *you heareth me;*"[6] "If he will not *hear
the church,* let him be unto thee as an heathen man."[7]
This my church went forth *in my name*—in the high
authority of my special commission : but thou wouldst
not re e it—thou wouldst not hear it: *another* church
car *in its own name*—neither sent nor commissioned
by me—*that church* thou hast both received and heard.

Thus, then, thou searchedst the Scriptures, *thinking*
to find therein eternal life : those Scriptures testified of
a perpetual, never-erring, teaching authority by me es-

[1] Matt. xvi, 18; Luke x, 16; Matt. xxviii, 20; John xiv, 16,
17; John xvi, 13; Isai. lix, 21; 1 Tim. iii, 15. [2] See note 1 on
page 11. [3] See first note on this page. [4] Matt. xviii, 17; Heb.
xiii, 7, 17; 2 Thes. ii, 15, compared with 2 Thes. iii, 14; Mark
xvi, 16. [5] John vii, 41, 42, 52; Matt. xxii, 23, 24. [6] Luke x,
16. [7] Matt. xviii, 17.

tablished; they directed thee to that teaching authority, if thou wouldst have life :[1] and yet, like the unbelieving Jews, thou *wouldst not follow* the testimony of the Scriptures; for thou wouldst not receive the authority of which they thus testified, but *protested against it.* Thou unbeliever! thou *Christian Jew!* from the very rule then, and the *very text* even, wherein thou hast trusted, and which thou thyself hast chosen — out of *thy own mouth* do I condemn thee.[2]

JUDAS *to the Catholic.*— And hast *thou* also protested against the church which I established? Hast *thou* also dared to *mistrust* and *gainsay* my infallible promises made to that church?

REASONS WHY THE CATHOLIC ADHERES TO THE CHURCH.

CATHOLIC.— LORD, far has it been from me, to sit in judgment upon the words of Eternal Truth, and pronounce them of *no effect.* For I knew and have believed, that *thy word* having once gone forth out of thy mouth, could not return unto thee *void,* without prospering in the thing whereunto thou didst send it.[3] Against that church, therefore, which thy words had established in perpetual truth, I have not presumed to protest — neither have I dared to mistrust or gainsay thy infallible promises made to it; but as *thou hast said,* so *I* have *believed.*

For I have believed *upon thy word,* in that very church which thou builtest upon a rock — in that " pillar and ground of the truth"[4]— because I knew that, by reason of thy word, the gates of hell could never prevail against it ;[5] and because thou didst threaten to rank me with the *very heathen,* if I should neglect to hear it.[6] *Upon thy word,* I have received the pastors of that church, as if I had received thyself: for I remembered thy solemn

[1] Heb. xiii, 7, 17; Mark xvi, 15, 16; Matt. xviii, 17. [2] Luke xix, 22. [3] Isai. lv, 11; Numbers xxiii, 19; Matthew xxiv, 35. [4] 1 Tim. iii, 15. [5] Matt. xvi, 18. [6] Matt. xviii, 17.

declaration, which saith, "Verily, verily, I say unto
you, he that receiveth whomsoever I send, receiveth
me."[1] Whom therefore thou hadst sent, to wit, thy
apostles and their successors, them have I received in
thy name; their united voice I have heard and obeyed;[2]
for I knew and have believed, that according to thy sure
promises, thou wast *always with them* in every age;[3] and
that the Spirit of Truth did *never cease* to abide with
them, to guide them into all truth;[4] thereby fulfilling
that which had been spoken concerning thy church by
Isaias the Prophet, when he said, " The Redeemer shall
come to Zión, and unto them that turn from transgres-
sion in Jacob, saith the Lord. As for me, this is my
covenant with them, saith the Lord, *My spirit* that is
upon thee, and *my words* which I have put in thy mouth,
*shall not depart out of thy mouth, nor out of the mouth
of thy seed, nor out of the mouth of thy seed's seed, saith
the Lord*, FROM HENCEFORTH AND FOR EVER."[5] Following thus thy words and relying upon thy promises,
I gave a willing ear to the teaching of thy church; and
received my faith from it, with the full assurance that
I was receiving the truth. And now, calling heaven
and earth to witness, confidently do I say, " LORD, *if in
this I have been deceived, it is thy very* OWN WORDS *that
have deceived me.*"

There came, indeed, *another church* and said to me,
" Lo, here is Christ."[6] And when this church had
quickly shot forth branches, and produced fruit *after its
own kind*, to wit, the fruit of dissent — each dissenting
church also came and said to me, " Lo, he is here." But
I believed them not;[7] for by their fruits I knew them;[8]
nor departed I from thy *divine* institution, to follow their
human inventions.

For, like those false teachers of whom the chief of

[1] John xiii, 20. [2] Luke x, 16; Heb. xiii, 7, 17; 2 Thess. ii, 15;
Matt. xviii, 17. [3] Matt. xxviii, 20. [4] John xiv, 16, 17; John
xvi, 13. [5] Isai. lix, 20, 21; Rom. xi, 26, 27. [6] Matt. xxiv, 23.
[7] Matt. xxiv, 26. [8] Matt. vii, 16, 20.

thy apostles had foretold, that they would bring in damnable heresies, even denying the Lord that bought them; that *many* would follow their pernicious ways, by reason of whom the way of truth would be evil spoken of; and that they would speak evil even of the things that they understood not :[1] so these *new* churches did bring in *strange* doctrines; and though they agreed not together in other things, yet, with one common voice, they all united to speak evil of the way of truth, to wit, of "the church of the living God, the pillar and ground of the truth." They denied even the plainest words of the Lord that bought them; for in nothing did thy divine words speak more plainly, than in showing the perpetual truth and authority of that church which they all denied, protesting against her and speaking evil of her doctrines — "things that they understood not." Pointing to her, they with one voice exclaimed: Lo! she is defiled with the filth of her corruptions and her abominations; she openeth her mouth in blasphemies, and teacheth men superstition, and impieties, and damnable idolatry! And herein they repeated against *thy spotless church* the same evil speaking as the unbelieving Jews had pronounced against *thyself.* "He deceiveth the people," they exclaimed; "He hath a devil, and is mad: why hear ye him?" "He hath spoken blasphemy; what further need have we of witnesses? Behold now ye have heard his blasphemy: What think ye? They answered and said, He is guilty of death."[2] When, therefore, I heard thy church also, whereof the Scriptures testified that she was "holy and without blemish,"[3] in like manner evil spoken of, I regarded it not: for I knew that from some wise dispensation of thy providence such had always been the lot of truth. I suffered not myself therefore to be led away with the error of the wicked; nor did I fall from mine own steadfastness:[4] but continued unto the end, to receive my

[1] 2 Pet. ii, 1, 2, 12.   [2] John vii, 12, John x, 20; Matt. xxvi, 65, 66.   [3] Eph. v 27.   [4] 2 Pet. iii, 17.

faith from that same never-failing source of truth whereunto thy words had conducted me.

Oft for this was *I*, in like manner, reviled and ridiculed — men laughed me to scorn[1] — but I heeded them not; for thy sure word was my guarantee. With the reviler sometimes did I behold the dearest of my friends;[2] and even they of mine own household became my foes.[3] But when I was reviled, I reviled not again,[4] because I would not render evil for evil, nor railing for railing, but contrariwise, blessing.[5] Yea, I rather rejoiced whenever I was counted worthy to suffer shame for thy name and for the truth.[6] For I remembered thy promise, " Blessed are ye when men shall revile you, and persecute you, and shall say *all manner of evil* against you *falsely* for my sake; rejoice and be exceeding glad: for great is your reward in heaven."[7] I called to mind also, what I have just before said — that *thou* didst first receive such treatment from men for my example; that the world — even thine own chosen people — *first* hated and persecuted thee:[8] that they *falsely accused,*[9] and *unjustly condemned* thee.[10] I therefore, like the church to which I was so inseparably attached, could look for no better treatment[11] — I desired no better: for, under all such treatment, I had comfort in that Scripture which saith, "whom God did foreknow, he also did predestinate to be *conformed to the image of his Son.*[12]

HIS FAITH APPROVED.

JUDGE *to the Catholic.* — " Blessed are they that have *heard* the word of God and *kept* it."[13] In that thou hast *believed* my words, thou hast done well; yet if thy faith hath been without works, it profiteth thee nothing:[14] but if, believing my words, thou hast *also done*

---

[1] Ps. xxii, 6, 7; Job xii, 4. [2] Ps. lv, 12. [3] Matt. x, 36. [4] 1 Pet. ii, 23. [5] 1 Pet. iii, 9. [6] Acts v, 41. [7] Matt. v, 11, 12; John xvi, 20, 22. [8] John xv, 18, 19, 20, 21, 25; Ps. xxii, 6, 7. [9] Mark xiv, 56, 57. [10] Mark xiv, 64, 65. [11] John xv, 20; John xiii, 16. [12] Rom. viii, 29. [13] Luke xi, 28. [14] James ii, 14.

them; then, blessed art thou: for thou shalt receive the crown of righteousness, which I, the righteous Judge, will give unto thee.[1]

REFLECTIONS ON THE PRECEDING CHAPTER.

Now, dear reader, let me entreat you to pause here awhile in order to give a few moments to serious reflection.

You have been taught from your infancy to look upon the *authority* which the Catholic church claims in her teaching, and upon the *character of never-failing truth* in her teaching, which she also claims, as being groundless assumptions and gross errors — you have been taught to *protest* against these claims as having no foundation in the Word of God — as being nothing better than popish corruptions.

You have just seen, however, that Christ has in plain words commissioned and *authorized* his church to teach,[2] and has given to its teaching *such authority*, that he will not suffer any one to "neglect to hear the church."[3] Ask yourself now the following very serious questions: "Should I like to be ranked *with heathens* at the day of judgment? And does not Christ say that those persons *are* to be ranked with heathens, who neglect to hear the church? and if this is to be the case with those that merely *neglect* to hear it, what will become of such as go so far as even to *protest against it?*"

You have seen also that Christ has, in the plainest manner, promised to the teaching of his church the *character of never-failing truth*, by having promised that "the gates of hell *shall not* prevail against it," for that he himself will *never cease* to be *with* its pastors, and that the spirit of truth will never cease to be with them also, and guide them in all truth.[4] Now, will you dare to say to Christ at the last day, that he did not make

[1] 2 Tim. iv, 7, 8. [2] See note 1, page 11. [3] See note 4, page 12. [4] See note 1, page 12.

18

these promises good? And yet you *do* say this, when
you *protest* against that church which he established —
as having fallen off from the truth, and become corrupted in her doctrines. For do you not thereby contradict
the very words of God — the clear promises of Christ
to his church? Oh! lay aside all prejudice. Reflect
seriously; for this is no trifling matter — it is no trifling
matter to disbelieve or disregard *any* of the words of
Christ. As far, indeed, as it is a matter between yourself and your fellow men, you may believe what you
please — you have liberty of conscience, *no man* having
a right to force the conscience of another: but as far as
it is a matter between yourself and your God, the case
is very different — you *may not* believe what you please
— you have no liberty of conscience whatever; for what
Christ has said, *that* you *must* believe, or suffer the consequences of your unbelief. And those consequences
are most terrible: for Christ has declared, — "He that
believeth not shall be damned." Now, he that believeth
not what? Why, evidently, those very doctrines which
he was *then* commissioning his apostles to teach — he
that believeth not *those very doctrines* (there is no exception) shall be damned.

That religion only, which the apostles taught, can be
the true one: all others, besides that one, must be *false
religions.* Now when Christ said, He that believeth not
shall be damned; he certainly did not mean to say, He
that believed not a *false religion* shall be damned; but
He that believeth not the one true religion. Whoever
therefore is not a member of the true religion, either
because he is *wilfully* ignorant of it, or because, *knowing
it,* he neglects to embrace it, does most certainly subject
himself to the terrible sentence of condemnation pronounced against those that believe not.[*]

This is a very serious consideration: for it shows how

* Amongst those that are in error, who they are that are
wilfully or *knowingly* so, it is not for man to determine, but for
Him who alone is the searcher of hearts.

important, and how necessary it is to discover, amidst
so many different religions — not which of them will
best suit your fancy, or your temporal interests — but
which of them is *that one* that was taught by the apostles; and to believe and practice it when discovered, for
upon this depends your eternal salvation.

EXAMINATION UPON INDIVIDUAL DOCTRINES.

It has been shown in the preceding chapter, from
clear and direct testimonies, that the church has a security from her divine Founder for the authority and perpetual truth of her teaching: and that this security is
nothing less than the *promises* of Him who declares,
that though heaven and earth shall pass away, yet his
word shall not pass away.[1] But, dear reader, if you
still think that the Catholic church *did* fall off from the
truth, and became grossly corrupted in her doctrines,
notwithstanding the plain and positive promises of Christ
to the contrary — let us now *try* a few of her doctrines,
such as are looked upon by Protestants and other dissenters as being very unscriptural and as damnable errors.

CHAPTER II.

ST. PETER'S SUPREMACY.

SUPPOSE, then, the Judge to address you again after
the following manner:

JUDGE *to the Protesting Christian.* — What is this
that thou hast done![2] I prayed to the Father that my
ministers and all the members of my church might be
united together in the bond of perfect union — that *they*
might be ONE as *He* and *I* are ONE.[3] And, as a means
of keeping them thus united, I gave to one of my apos-

tles a *supremacy* over the rest — over the whole church.'
Why hast *thou* declared against his appointment? Why
hast *thou* presumed to *protest* against his authority?

GROUNDS OF A PROTEST SOUGHT FOR IN SCRIPTURE.

PROTESTING CHRISTIAN. — Lord, in support of such
appointment I could find no warranty of Holy Scriptures, but the contrary; and therefore did I *protest*
against it. For, how could I believe that one of thy
apostles was made superior to another, when I found
the Scriptures testifying that the same power was given
to them all? The power of *binding* and *loosing*, though
at first given individually to Peter,[1] was afterwards ex-
tended to the whole collective body of the apostles.[2]
The Scriptures told me, that the faithful were built upon
the foundation of the apostles and prophets, *thou thyself*
being the chief corner-stone.[3] The great apostle of the
gentiles declared, that "in nothing was he behind the
very *chiefest* apostles."[4] And of this he gave a practical
proof at Antioch, by withstanding Peter to the face,
because he was to be blamed.[5] And besides all this,
thou thyself didst teach me, that in thy church no one
was to be chief, nor to exercise lordship over the rest:
"Ye shall not be so, thou didst say: but he that is
greatest among you, let him be as the younger; and he
that is chief, as he that doth serve."[6]

THE VERY TEXTS QUOTED FOR, PLEAD AGAINST THE
PROTEST.

JUDGE. — Out of thine own mouth will I condemn
thee![7] Thou wicked servant! in this also thou hast
imitated the unbelieving Jews. For, although the books
of the Old Law gave testimony *of me*, yet such testimony the Jews *would not* find therein; but they found
sundry words which they wrested from their proper

[1] Matt. xvi, 19. [2] Matt. xviii, 18. [3] Eph. ii, 19, 20. [4] 2 Cor.
xii, 11. [5] Gal. ii, 11. [6] Luke xxii, 25, 26. [7] Luke xix, 22.

meaning, so as to give them an *appearance* of bearing testimony *against me*. And herein they fulfilled the prophecy of Isaias, which saith, "This people's heart is waxed gross, and their ears are dull of hearing, and *their eyes they have closed; lest* at any time they should see with their eyes, and hear with their ears, and should understand with their heart, *and be converted*, and I should heal them."[1] So, likewise, although the books of the New Law gave the clearest testimony of *Peter's supremacy*,[2] yet *thou* couldst not — *because thou wouldst not* — find therein such testimony; but thou couldst find certain passages, which, when turned from their plain and proper sense, had *some appearance* of testifying *against* his supremacy : And thus, with the Scriptures in thy hand, like the Jews of old, seeing, thou wouldst not see, and reading, thou wouldst not understand; but hast closed thine eyes against the truth, and blinded thine understanding, LEST *thou shouldst be converted :* Like them, thou hast wrested the Scriptures unto thine own destruction.[3] All this I will now make clear :

The power of binding and loosing was, indeed, given to all my apostles together, Peter being then amongst them; but this power I gave in a more *marked* manner to Peter *singly and individually*. For to *him*, but to none of the rest, did I accompany it with the promise, that I would "give the keys of the kingdom of heaven."[3] Again, the faithful were built upon the foundation of all my apostles, Peter amongst the rest; but I promised to build my church upon Peter *individually* and in a more special manner.[4] And thus, in these two instances, I showed most clearly, that *all* of them, indeed, were perfectly apostles and ministers; but that respecting Peter there was something *individual, and special, and*

[1] Matt. xiii, 13, 14, 15.　[2] 2 Peter iii, 16.　[3] Matthew xvi, 19.
[4] Matthew xvi, 18.

superior: Just in the same manner as when it was declared of *all* my apostles together, that *I loved them;*[1] but of John individually, that he was "*the disciple whom Jesus loved;*"[2] it was thereby plainly signified, that, in my love for him, there was something special and superior: as also, when I called all men collectively to "follow me,"[3] but said to my *apostles* individually, "*follow me;*"[4] I thereby showed that *they* were to follow me in a *more special manner* than the rest of mankind. So far, therefore, thy appeals to Scripture stand against thee — thy *apparent* testimony *against* Peter's supremacy is, in truth, *real* testimony *for* it.

When my apostle of the gentiles said he was "in nothing behind the very chiefest apostles,"[5] it was evident that he was speaking only of what was *essential to the apostleship*, showing that, though not one of the twelve, yet he was as much *an apostle* as even the *very chiefest* of them; but he was not speaking of *peculiur* and *individual* privileges, such as were not essential to the apostleship. This was manifest from the words "very chiefest," whereby he plainly taught that there was some pre-eminence amongst them.

Nor was the fact of his having "withstood Peter to the face"[6] a proof that Peter possessed no pre-eminence, any more than the fact of one of a king's ministers withstanding the *prime minister* to the face, for acting imprudently, would be a proof that such prime minister enjoyed no degree of pre-eminence over the other. But rather, would not the very recording of such an occurrence, as a courageous or bold act, sufficiently indicate that the prime minister was considered to be something superior to the other?

When teaching humility, I told my apostles, that the kings of the gentiles exercised lordship over men, but that *they* should not be so; my meaning evidently was,

---

[1] John xv, 9, 12, 13, 14; John xiii, 1. [2] John xix, 26; John xxi, 7, 20. [3] Luke ix, 23; Luke xiv, 27. [4] Matt. iv, 18, 19, 20. [5] 2 Cor. xii, 11. [6] Gal. ii, 11.

that they should not use any authority or pre-eminence, which they might have in a proud and domineering manner, like the kings of the gentiles. And when I said, "He that is greatest among you, let him be as the younger; and he that is chief, as he that doth serve;"[1] I plainly taught that there was *one greatest — one chief* — among them; but that he was to act with as much humility *as if* he were the servant of the rest; therein following my example, who, though supreme head of the church and *in all things pre-eminent*,[2] was among them nevertheless, *as he* that served.[3]

Thus, then, even those very same words of Scripture whereunto thou hast appealed to justify thy protest, *all* plead against thee; so that out of thine own mouth it is that I condemn thee.

JUDGE *to the Catholic.* — And hast *thou*, in like manner, withdrawn thyself from that Supremacy — that centre of unity — which I established in my church? Hast *thou* also presumed to *protest* against it?

REASONS WHY THE CATHOLIC ADMITS PETER'S SUPREMACY.

CATHOLIC. — Lord, so clearly and so explicitly did thy sacred words establish that supremacy in thy church, that I could not have protested against it, without *feeling conscious* that I was protesting against a *divine* institution.

Thou thyself wast the foundation and chief cornerstone of the church.[4] But, knowing that thou wouldst shortly withdraw from the earth thy *visible presence*, and not willing to leave thy church, which was a *visible* establishment,[5] without a *visible* foundation or chief corner-stone, thou didst appoint Peter to be in this respect, *thy vicegerent* on earth: For, having changed his name from Simon to Peter, thou didst afterwards make

[1] Luke xxii, 25, 26.   Col. 1, 18.   [3] Luke xxii, 27.   [4] 1 Cor. iii, 11; Eph. ii, 20.   [5] Isaias ii, 2, 3, and Micah iv, 1, 2, compared with Matt. v, 14, 15.

to *him*, but to none of the rest, this positive declaration. "I say unto thee that thou art Peter (i. e. *a rock*,) and *upon this rock I will build my church;* and the gates of hell shall not prevail against it."[1] This promise, made thus *individually and solely* to Peter, constrained me to acknowledge in him something *special,— some pre-eminence in the church,* above the rest of the apostles.

Again, thou didst possess the *keys* of the kingdom of heaven, to wit, supreme authority in the church; for, of thee it was aforetold, that thou shouldst have the key of the house of David; that thou shouldst open and none should shut, thou shouldst shut and none should open.[2] Now, in this character also, thou didst constitute Peter thy vicegerent on earth: For thou didst communicate to *him* individually and singly this self same power, saying: "I give unto THEE the keys of the kingdom of heaven; and whatsoever thou shalt bind on earth, shall be bound in heaven; and whatsoever thou shalt loose on earth, shall be loosed in heaven."[3] This power of the keys being thus given singly and specially to Peter, also obliged me to recognize in *him* some special power in the church, above the rest of the apostles.

Again, thou wast the supreme shepherd over the whole flock — over both clergy and laity: thou wast the *one shepherd* of the *one sheep-fold.*[4] And in this character also, thou didst constitute Peter thy *vicegerent* on earth: For, after thy resurrection, thou didst commission *him,* but none of the rest, to feed thy *whole flock,* sheep and lambs, to wit, clergy and laity; saying to him — Simon, son of Jonas, lovest thou me MORE *than these?* He said, Yea, Lord; thou knowest that I love thee. Thou saidst unto him, Feed my lambs. Thou saidst to him again a second and a third time, Simon, son of Jonas, lovest thou me? He said, Yea, Lord; thou knowest that I love thee. Twice thou saidst unto him, Feed my

[1] Matthew xvi, 18. [2] Isaias xxii, 22, compared with Rev. iii, 7. [3] Matthew xvi, 19. [4] John x, 11, 14, 16; Hebrews xiii, 20; 1 Peter v, 4.

sheep.[1] Now, the circumstance of Peter being thus required to love thee *more* than the others, manifestly showed, that upon him was conferred some special and higher privilege — some *more responsible* charge that required on his part a greater pledge of fidelity; for, otherwise, it would have been sufficient if he had loved *as much* as the rest. This circumstance, then, as well as the plain *fact* of his having been here appointed *the one* or *supreme shepherd* over thy *whole flock*, forced me again to acknowledge in him a pre-eminence over the whole church; and obliged me, if I would be one of thy flock, to submit to *him* as my *visible* supreme shepherd; Thou thyself being the supreme *invisible* shepherd of my soul.

Again, on another occasion, and in another character, thou didst commission Peter to act as thy *vicegerent* on earth; and didst expressly mention, that this office was to be exercised by him over his fellow apostles: For unto him thou saidst, "Simon, Simon, behold Satan hath desired to have *you* (apostles,) that he may sift *you* as wheat; but I have prayed for THEE, that thy faith fail not; and when thou art converted, *strengthen thy brethren*."[2] All thy apostles, going forth as thy ministers, were to establish the kingdom of thy church, and thereby to overthrow the kingdom of satan. In order to prevent such overthrow, satan desired to have thy apostles in his power, (satan hath desired to have *you*.) But, to frustrate his malignant designs against all thy apostles, thou prayedst — not for them all — but for *Peter only*, that his faith might not fail, (but I have prayed for *thee*:) and having thus strengthened *him* in faith, thou didst not thyself strengthen the others, but didst commit that office unto Peter, to be exercised by him, after he had risen from his fall (and when thou art converted, *strengthen thy brethren*; that is to say, do *thou* strengthen *them* as *I* have strengthened *thee*.) Here, then, I was again, a fourth time, compelled to acknow-

[1] John xxi, 15, 16, 17. [2] Luke xxii, 31.

ledge in Peter a pre-eminence or supremacy over all the rest.

Since, then, in all these various characters and offices, thou didst so clearly and so explicitly commission Peter to act as thy *vicegerent* on earth, I have acknowledged his supremacy. For I could not have protested against it, without feeling conscious that I was thereby contradicting and blaspheming thy sacred and infallible words.[1] Again, therefore, may I confidently call heaven and earth to witness,[2] that if in this I have been deceived, it is thy very *own words* that have deceived me : for, as *thou* hast said, so *I* have *believed.*

THE BELIEF OF THE SUPREMACY APPROVED.

JUDGE *to the Catholic.*— Blessed art thou, because thou hast not been *"faithless* but believing!"[3] So far hast thou faithfully received, and steadfastly believed " every word that hath proceeded out of my mouth;"[4] so far, therefore, my justice and my truth record sentence in thy favor.

THE PROTEST AGAINST IT CONDEMNED.

JUDGE, *turning now to the Protesting Christian*—But thou wicked, thou' *faithless* servant! thou *Christian Jew!* Thou searchedst the Scriptures; for in them *thou thoughtest* thou hadst eternal life,[5] in protesting against Peter's *supremacy;* and the Scriptures were they that thus clearly testified of it; and though they so plainly testified of it, yet thou *wouldst not believe it;* but *protestedst against it.* The Scriptures, then — thine own chosen rule — are they that accuse thee, and condemn thee.[6]

[1] Acts xiii, 45. [2] Deut. iv, 26. [3] John xx, 27. [4] Matt. iv, 4. [5] John v, 39. [6] John v, 45.

CHAPTER III.

INVOCATION OF ANGELS AND SAINTS.

But I have something yet further against thee! In my church I established a perfect "Communion of Saints."[1] For, not only did I appoint that my servants on earth should intercede one for another, but I also established a *mutual intercourse* between my angels and saints who incessantly adored before my throne in heaven, and the members of my church on earth. Why hast thou protested against that mutual intercourse — against that "Communion of Saints" which I had thus established?

REASONS FOR THE PROTEST AGAINST SUCH INVOCATION.

Protesting Christian. — Lord, in the Holy Scriptures I thought I had sufficient ground for such a protest. For they told me, that "there was *one mediator* between God and men; *the man Christ Jesus*, who gave himself a ransom for all;"[2] and that "no man came unto the Father but by thee;"[3] for that "there was none other name under heaven given among men whereby we must be saved."[4] If, then, I had sought any other way of coming to the Father, except by thee, — if I had supplicated the angels and saints, for their prayers or intercession, this would have been doing injury to thy mediatorship, — it would have been the same as denying its sufficiency: and, moreover, it would have been quite useless, because the angels and saints could neither hear nor help so many persons praying to them at the same time, unless they had been omnipresent and omniscient; and so far were the *saints*, or persons *after death*, from being omnipresent and omniscient, that, according to

[1] Apostles' Creed. [2] 1 Tim. ii, 5, 6. [3] John xiv, 6. [4] Acts iv, 12.

the Scripture, "the *dead* know not any thing, neither have they any more a reward, for *the memory of them is forgotten.*"[1]

THE PROTEST STANDS SELF-CONDEMNED.

JUDGE *to the Protesting Christian.* — Thou hast pronounced thine own condemnation! When my apostle said, "There is *one mediator* between God and men, the man Christ Jesus," he immediately explained what kind of mediator he was then speaking of — "There is one mediator, he said, *who gave himself a ransom for all;*"[2] to wit, there is but one mediator *who ransomed men* — but one mediator by redemption. He taught, therefore, that *I alone* could stand between God and men to obtain blessings for them, on the title of having *purchased* them by giving myself "a ransom for all." In this sense, then, he taught that I was the *only* mediator. And it was also in the same sense that he spoke when he said: "There is none other name under heaven given among men whereby they must be saved."[3] For, unless mankind had been *redeemed, none* could have been saved; and, as *I alone* redeemed them, it was therefore *by me alone* that they were saved: and thus it was that "no man came unto the Father *but by me,*"[4] to wit, but *by the redemption* which I purchased for them.

But, though I was the *only one* who gave myself a *ransom* for thee — the only mediator *by redemption;* — though I was the only one who could interpose mine *own merits* in thy favor; may there not have been other beings who could *intercede* in thy behalf — not indeed by redemption — not through any independent merits of *their own* — but through *my infinite merits?*[*] or may

[1] Eccl. ix, 5. [2] 1 Tim. ii, 5, 6. [3] Acts iv, 10, 12. [4] John xiv, 6.

[*] This is exactly the Catholic doctrine on the Invocation of Angels and Saints. It is solely *through the merits of Christ, our only Redeemer*, that such invocation is made. For, what the Catholic church teaches is this — "That the Saints, who reign

there not have been beings who could *ask me* to mediate
for thee, without either injuring my mediatorship, or
denying its sufficiency? Thou hast said *not*, and in so
saying, hast pronounced judgment against thyself.

For thou thyself hast believed, (and such belief was
in accordance with Scripture,) that the faithful on earth
might pray and *intercede* one for another, and might ask
each other's intercession.[1] Indeed, in the beginning of
that very chapter wherein I was called the "one mediator," did I not inspire my apostle to teach, that there
might be *other intercessors* between God and men? "I
exhort, he said, that first of all, supplications, prayers,
intercessions, and giving of thanks, be made FOR *all
men.*"[2] Now, was not this making the faithful *intercessors between God and their fellow men?* And whether
these intercessors were on earth or in heaven at the time
of their interceding, could it make any difference whatever, *as far as regarded any injury done by them to my
mediatorship?* In this respect, was it not exactly the
same in both cases? for, in both cases, it was *an inter-*

[1] 1 Sam. vii, 8; Job xlii, 8; Eph. vi, 18, 19; 1 Thess. v, 25;
James v, 16. [2] 1 Tim. ii, 1.

with Christ, offer up their prayers to God for men; that it is
good and profitable suppliantly to invoke them, and to have
recourse to their prayers and assistance, in order to obtain
blessings *from God, through his Son Jesus Christ our Lord, who
is our only Redeemer and Saviour."* (*Con. Trid. Sess. XXV.
De Invocatione.*)

The act of invocating the Angels and Saints is frequently
called "idolatrous," by those who protest against the Catholic
church. Now, idolatry is *giving God's honor or God's worship
to creatures:* and Catholics are accused of doing this, when they
invoke the Saints. How low in intellect, or how enslaved to
prejudice must that man be, who can seriously make this accu-
sation! Catholics ask the Angels and Saints to *pray for them:*
can *that* be giving them God's honor or God's worship? Is it the
honor or worship *belonging to God,* to ask *Him* to *pray for us?*
So far, indeed, from this being an *adoration* of God, would it
not be plainly *denying him to be God?* And yet the Catholics
are gravely accused of making gods of the Saints, when they
ask the Saints to *pray for them!*

ceding between God and men — in both cases, it was equally having recourse to *other intercessors* besides me. To the members of my church thou saidst: "Why ask the Angels and Saints to pray for you, as if your Saviour — the one mediator — were not sufficient?" The same thing will I now say to thee: "Why ask thy fellow sinners on earth to pray for thee, as if thy Saviour — the one mediator — were not sufficient? or, as if the prayers of thy fellow sinners on earth were more acceptable to me than the prayers of my Angels and Saints in heaven?" What answer canst thou make, except that thou hast herein condemned thyself?

But thou hast said, the Angels and Saints in heaven could not hear nor help so many persons that might be praying to them at once, without being omnipresent and omniscient. And hast *thou*, then — the mere creature of my hands — presumed to measure thy Creator's power! to set bounds to my divine Omnipotence! Wilt thou dare to tell *me* to my face, that I was not sufficiently powerful to make them know the prayers of thousands and millions of supplicants from different parts of the earth, without rendering them omnipresent and omniscient? Thou didst not believe ME, *as man*, to be omnipresent; for, when objecting to my real presence in that sacrament of love which I instituted the night before my passion, thou saidst that that sacrament could not be my real body, because my real body, thou saidst, could not be on so many altars at the same time. But, though I was not, *as man* omnipresent, yet, did I not, *as man*, hear the prayers of all that prayed to me? for, was it not *as man* that I was the *one mediator* — "*the* MAN *Christ Jesus?*"

But, to prove that the Saints *knew not* who prayed to them, thou hast appealed to the Scriptures of the Old Law, which said: "The dead know not any thing, neither have they any more a reward, for the memory of them is forgotten."[1] It was evident that this was not

[1] Eccles. ix, 5.

spoken of departed *saints*, but of *sinners;* because David said, "The *righteous* shall be (not forgotten, but) in everlasting remembrance:"[1] but "the face of the Lord is against them that do evil, to cut off the remembrance *of them* from the earth."[2] And another Scripture said, "The memory of *the just* is blessed; but the name of *the wicked* shall rot."[3] It was evident also, that it could not have been spoken of saints *in heaven, or reigning with me;* because it was spoken of the dead some hundreds of years before I had purchased man's redemption, and therefore of persons *not* in heaven; for none entered into heaven before their redemption had been purchased.[4] It was evident, therefore, that it could be no proof whatever, that *saints when in heaven* or reigning with me, knew nothing.

Indeed, that they and the angels *did* know things passing on earth, and even took an interest therein, the Scriptures clearly taught thee, but thou wouldst not believe their teaching. For, when I admonished the Jews, saying, "Take heed that ye despise not one of these little ones; for I say unto you, that in heaven their angels do always behold the face of my Father who is in heaven,"[5] did not the threat contained in these last words manifestly show, that when little ones were despised on earth, their angels in heaven knew it? The same truth I also taught in the parable of the lost sheep. For, as the shepherd rejoiced at finding the sheep that had been lost, I declared that in like manner there was joy in the presence of the angels of God over one sinner that repented.[6] The repentance of sinners, therefore, was known to the angels; otherwise, it could not have been to them a subject of joy. But, if they could know the *repentance* of the heart, could they not also know the *requests* of the heart? and if they *rejoiced* over repenting sinners, did they not take an interest in their welfare?

[1] Ps. cxli, 6. [2] Ps. xxxiv, 16. [3] Prov. x, 7. [4] John iii, 13; Heb. xi, 39, 40. [5] Matt. xviii, 10; Mark ix, 42; See Ps. xxxiv, 7. [6] Luke xv, 7, 10.

Now, what was thus said of the angels was equally applicable to the *saints in heaven;* for so I expressly taught, saying, they " are *as* the angels of God in heaven ;"[1] " for they are *equal* unto the angels."[2] And this I taught still more explicitly in the revelation which I made to my beloved disciple, saying : " He that overcometh, and *keepeth my works unto the end,* to *him* will I give *power over the nations,* and he shall *rule them* with a rod of iron."[3] This was evidently spoken of saints — of those who had not only *kept my works,* but had kept them *unto the end;* and consequently of saints *after they had finished their mortal life.* These words, then, made it manifest, that the *saints* in heaven *must* have known what passed on earth among *the nations,* and must also have interested themselves therein; otherwise, how could they have been said to exercise power over the nations — to *rule* the nations? What answer canst thou make, except that, like the unbelieving Sadducees, thou hast " erred, not knowing the Scriptures, nor the power of God ;"[4] and that, in all thy protests, thou hast wrested the Scriptures unto thine own destruction ;[5] contradicting and blaspheming my sacred word ?[6]

A FURTHER REASON FOR THE PROTEST.

PROTESTING CHRISTIAN. — Lord, why doth thy wrath wax hot against me,[7] seeing thy conduct towards the *Virgin Mary* at the marriage feast of Cana was such, as sufficiently to prove to me, that she was not intended to be my intercessor? For the manner in which thou didst treat her request on that occasion, plainly indicated a rejection of her intercession : for, no sooner had she signified her request by saying, " They have no wine," than thou saidst unto her : " Woman, what have I to do with thee? mine hour is not yet come."[8]

[1] Matt. xxii, 30. [2] Luke xx, 36. [3] Rev. ii, 26, 27. [4] Matt. xxii, 29. [5] 2 Peter iii, 16. [6] Acts xiii, 45. [7] Exod. xxxii, 11. [8] John ii, 3, 4.

A FURTHER CONDEMNATION OF THE PROTEST.

JUDGE *to Protesting Christian.* — Thou hast only added to thy condemnation. Mary having been chosen to be the Mother of *me*,[1] who came to redeem the world, was styled by my angel "Blessed among women."[2] And she herself prophesied, saying, (speaking of course of the *true faithful,*) "From henceforth *all* generations *shall call me* BLESSED."[3] But thou and all thy protesting brethren, have carefully abstained from ever, or scarcely ever, giving her that title; showing thereby, that *you* were not of the number of those of whom she prophesied.

But, as to the manner in which I treated her request, so far was it from proving that I rejected her intercession, that on the contrary, nothing could more clearly prove *its efficacy;* since I even wrought a miracle on that occasion, in order to grant her request; although I had declared that the time for manifesting myself to the world by miracles was not then come. When they wanted wine, she (to signify her request that I would supply some by my divine power) said unto me, *they have no wine.*[4] And I (to show the difficulty of granting her request, as being opposed to the order of divine Providence) said unto her, *Woman, what have I to do with thee? mine hour is not yet come;*[5] (to wit, for manifesting myself to the world by working miracles. Yet so confident was she of her request being granted, that) she said unto the servants, *Whatsoever he saith unto you, do it. And there were set there six water-pots of stone — containing two or three firkins a piece.*[6] (Now, although I had declared that mine hour was not then come for granting her request by working a miracle, yet, seeing she persevered, I granted it; for) I said unto them, *Fill the water-pots with water. And they filled them up to the*

[1] Luke i, 31, 32, 35, 43; Luke ii, 7, 11; John ii, 1, 3, 5, 12; John xix, 25, 26; Acts i, 14. [2] Luke i, 28. [3] Luke i, 48.

*brim. And I said unto them, Draw out now and bear
unto the governor of the feast. And they bare it.*[1] And
it was found to be wine, as she had requested.[2]

The efficacy, then, of her intercession I could not
have shown in a clearer and more striking manner than
I did on that occasion. This thy last appeal, therefore,
whereby thou hast endeavored to justify thy protest,
like all the rest, pleads against thee; for herein thou
hast again wrested the Scriptures, as the unlearned and
unstable have always done, unto thine own destruction.[3]

JUDGE *turning to the Catholic.*—And hast *thou* also
protested against that mutual intercourse which was
carried on between my angels and saints in heaven, and
my servants on earth—against that mutual interchange
of good offices — that "communion of saints," which
existed in my church?

REASONS WHY THE CATHOLIC BELIEVES AND PRACTICES
THIS DOCTRINE.

CATHOLIC. — Lord, so far from protesting against it,
I have, on the contrary, suffered many a bitter scoff and
uncharitable reproach for having believed and practiced
it. This belief and practice I learned — not only from
the authoritative teaching of thy never-erring church,
whose teaching was, of itself, a sufficient testimony of
truth, resting as it did on thy infallible promises[4] — but
also from the plain teaching of the Holy Scriptures,
wherein I found it clearly stated, That *angels* in heaven
have prayed to God *in behalf of people on earth,* and by
such prayers *have obtained mercy;* and that the *saints*
in heaven also *prayed;* and I found it therein further
stated, That some of thy greatest servants on earth *have
invoked* angels, and *obtained* their requests; and that
the *saints* also offered *our prayers* to God. So that I
could not have believed otherwise than I have done on

[1] John ii, 7, 8. [2] John ii, 9. [3] 2 Pet. iii, 16. [4] See note 1,
page 11; note 1, page 12; note 4, page 12.

this subject, without feeling conscious that the Holy Scriptures contained and would pronounce my condemnation.

First. *That the Blessed in Heaven do pray for us.*— For I found, in the Old Testament, thy prophet Zacharias relating this fervent and successful prayer of an angel: "Then the angel of the Lord answered and said, O Lord of hosts, how long wilt thou not have mercy on Jerusalem, and on the cities of Judah, against which thou hast had indignation these three-score and ten years? And the Lord answered the angel that talked with me, with good words and comfortable words...... Therefore, thus saith the Lord, *I am returned to Jerusalem with mercies.*"[1] Thus, then, I found thy sacred inspired word clearly and positively declaring, that an angel *did*, on that occasion, *intercede* for thy people,— *did* implore mercy in their behalf; and that the Lord answered the angel *favorably*, by actually showing the mercy which the angel had *prayed for*. These words, therefore, of Holy Scripture, not only *authorized*, but *obliged* me to believe that the blessed in heaven were intercessors for thy people on earth.

I found in the New Testament also, evidence equally strong to the same effect. For, *concerning the angels*, thou inspiredst thy beloved disciple to say: "I saw seven angels which stood before God......And another angel came and stood at the altar, having a golden censer; and there was given unto him much incense, that he should offer it with the *prayers of all saints* upon the golden altar which was before the throne. And the smoke of the incense which came with the *prayers* of the saints, ascended up, before God, *out of the angel's hand.*"[2] And to show that the same kind office was also performed by the *saints* in heaven — that *they* in like manner took part in this "communion of saints," the same apostle was inspired to say: "Round about the throne were four and twenty seats; and upon the

[1] Zach. I, 12, 13, 16.   [2] Rev. viii, 2, 3, 4.

seats I saw four and twenty elders sitting, clothed in white raiment; and they had on their heads crowns of gold.... And the four and twenty elders *fell down before the Lamb*, having every one of them harps, and golden vials *full of odors*, WHICH ARE THE PRAYERS OF SAINTS. And they sung a new song, saying, Thou art worthy to take the book, and to open the seals thereof; for thou wast slain, and hast *redeemed us* (hence these elders were *not* angels but saints) to God by thy blood, *out of every kindred, and tongue, and people, and nation.*"[1]

Now, in the former of these two declarations of thy sacred word, I found an ANGEL described as standing *near thy throne* and *offering up*, from his own hand, incense with the *prayers* of saints: and, in the latter, I found the SAINTS *around thy throne* spoken of as *falling down before thee*, having at the same time vials *filled with odors* and that those odors were THE PRAYERS OF SAINTS. Again, therefore, thy sacred and infallible words obliged me to believe, that both angels and saints in heaven *offered prayers* to thee, — presenting themselves before thee as intercessors; and that to the prayers of thy servants on earth, they also joined the incense of their own.

SECOND. *That we may ask the Blessed in Heaven to pray for us.*— And that it was both *lawful and profitable* for thy servants on earth to *invoke* these blessed spirits, thy sacred word gave equally clear and strong testimony. For it testified, that when the two angels, sent to destroy Sodom, were conducting Lot out of that city, he prayed to one of them, saying: " I cannot escape to the mountain, lest some evil take me, and I die. Behold now, this city (*Zoar*) is near to flee unto, and it is a little one: Oh let me escape thither, (is it not a little one?) and my soul shall live. And he (the angel) said unto him: See, I have accepted thee concerning this thing also, that I will not overthrow this city, for which thou hast spoken. Haste thee, escape thither;

[1] Rev. iv, 4, and Rev. v, 8, 9.

for I cannot do any thing till thou be come thither."[1]
Here, then, I found *supplication made* to an angel, and
the request *obtained.*

Thy servant Jacob also prayed to an angel — to the
angel with whom he had wrestled — saying to him: "I
will not let thee go, except thou bless me ; . . . . and he
blessed him there."[2] And thy prophet Hosea, after relating that Jacob "had power over the angel, and prevailed," expressly said, "He wept and *made supplication unto him.*"[3] Here, again, I found *supplication made*
to an angel, and a *blessing obtained.*

And when that same holy patriarch was sick, and
near his end, he called unto him the two sons of Joseph
to bless them: and when he blessed them, he *invoked* in
their behalf both *God* and *his guardian angel,* saying:
"God, before whom my fathers Abraham and Isaac did
walk, the God which fed me all my life long unto this
day ; *the angel which redeemed me from all evil, bless the
lads; and let my name be named on them.*"[4] Here then,

---

[1] Gen. xix, 1, 19, 20, 21, 22. [2] Gen. xxxii, 26, 29. [3] Hosea
xii, 4. [4] Gen. xlviii, 1, 9, 15, 16.

* To escape the force of the texts wherein Lot and Jacob are
described as praying to *angels,* some of our protesting brethren
say, that the angels which appeared and spoke to the ancient
Patriarchs, and also to Moses in the bush and on Mount Sinai,
were *not angels,* but *God — the promised Messiah.* But, to show
that they "*do err, not knowing the Scriptures,*" we need only
open the New Testament. For, in Acts vii, 30, 35, 38, it is
thrice plainly declared, that it was — *not the Lord* — but "an
angel of the Lord," that *appeared to Moses in the bush.* That
angel did, indeed, speak as God would speak; because he spoke
in God's name, and *as God's representative.* As to the giving
of the law, it is written, that it was given, not by God *person-
ally,* but by the ministry of *angels.* For St. Stephen says, the
Jews "received the law by the disposition *of angels.*" (Acts
vii, 53.) St. Paul also declares the same: "The law, he says,
was added because of transgressions . . . . . it was ordained *by
angels* in the hand of a mediator," viz. Moses. (Gal. iii, 19.)
The same apostle, after having shown that the angels are inferior to Christ, infers therefrom that the Old Law is inferior to
the New; because the former, he argues, was "*spoken by an-*

I found that venerable patriarch, for the purpose of obtaining a blessing from heaven, praying on his death-bed — not only to God — but also to an *angel* — to the angel who, during life, had rescued him from evil; and that angel was not represented as being then visibly present. I could not, and dared not, charge that holy and venerable patriarch with committing an idolatrous act on his death-bed; nor with doing any thing, on that solemn occasion, but what was *good and lawful*. But, if it was good and lawful in *him* to invoke the Blessed in heaven, I was obliged to believe that it could not be otherwise than good and lawful in *me* also to invoke them. And if Jacob and Lot invoked them with *benefit to themselves*, I had positive reason for believing, that it might be *beneficial to me* also, unless my unworthiness had put an obstacle in the way of such benefit. Again, therefore, do I confidently say: Lord, if in my belief on this subject I have been deceived, it is thy own sacred word that has deceived me.

JUDGE *to the Catholic*. — "Well done, good and *faithful* servant:[1] for thou hast chosen the way of truth.[2] And blessed art thou; because thou hast made to thyself friends, who, now that others have failed, shall, if thy works have been in accordance with thy faith, receive thee into everlasting habitations.[3]

REFLECTIONS ON CHAPTERS II. AND III.

Here again, dear reader, a few reflections will naturally present themselves to your mind:

[1] Matt. xxv, 23.   [2] Ps. cxix, 30.   [3] Luke xvi, 9.

gels," but the latter was "*spoken by the Lord*." (Heb. ii, 2, 3, 4.) For he had just before said, that it was not till "*these last days*," (i. e. the days of the Christian revelation,) that "*God hath spoken to us by his Son*." (Heb. i, 1, 2.)

Thus, then, the New Testament is clear on this subject. The evidence it gives, that *the angel* or *angels* spoken of in the books of Moses, were *not God*—*not Christ*, but really *angels*, is plain and positive. For St. Paul actually builds an argument upon the very circumstance that they *were* angels.

You have been brought up in the idea that the *doctrines* of the Catholic Church concerning the *invocation of angels and saints, and the supremacy of St. Peter*, are not to be met with in the Word of God; and you have been taught to protest against them as "the corruptions of popery." But, beware how you proceed in such a protest — pause — reflect. For, have you not just seen that these doctrines *are* contained *most clearly* in the sacred Scriptures; and therefore, that they are — *not corruptions* — but doctrines TAUGHT BY GOD HIMSELF, and consequently *to be believed* by every Christian? Perhaps *you* may think the disbelieving these doctrines to be a matter of no very great consequence; but, when God has taught *any* doctrine — whatever that doctrine may be — can it be a matter of small consequence *positively to disbelieve it?* and not disbelieve only, but absolutely to *protest against it as a* CORRUPTION? For, by so protesting, do you not fall under that terrible wo pronounced by the prophet Isaias: "Wo unto them that call *good evil*; .... that put *darkness* for *light?*" (Isa. v, 20.) For, when you protest against doctrines so clearly revealed by God, and pronounce them "corruptions," and when you substitute falsehoods for divine truths; do you not literally "call good evil," and "put darkness for light?" Beware, then, I again repeat it — beware how you proceed in such a protest. Reflect seriously: for the consequences are *eternal!*

A RECAPITULATION AS PRELIMINARY TO A FURTHER EXAMEN.

From the words of our blessed Redeemer, recorded in the Holy Scriptures and laid before you in the preceding pages, it is evident that he established a church on earth, and gave it authority and commission to teach in his name unto the end of the world; that he directs all who would be his disciples, to the teaching of this his church, requiring them to hear it, as they would hear himself; and that they who will not hear it, are to be accounted no better than *heathen* men. It is evident, moreover, that that church which he had thus established — that "pillar and ground of the truth" — was *never* to be deprived of the guidance of the Holy Spirit — was *never* to be prevailed against by the powers of darkness — was *never* to fall off from the truth, being secured therefrom by the clear and infallible promises of its divine Founder. (See Chap. I, pages 5, 6, 13, 14.)

Already has it been shown, from the plain and positive testimony of God's word, that *two* of the doctrines of the Catholic church, which Protesting Christians are accustomed to point at as "corruptions," and consequently, as *evidences* that she *has* fallen off from the truth, are in fact *not* "corruptions," but the *very doctrines of God's revelation.* (See Chap. II, pages 21; 23 to 27; and Chap. III, pages 27; 34 to 38.)

THE NEXT POINT WHEREON JUDGMENT PROCEEDS.

Although what has been already said, in the three preceding Chapters, is more than sufficient to show the *injustice* and *criminality* of the protest, which is so perseveringly carried on against the Catholic church; yet will we examine one subject more, because prejudice against it runs very high — I mean the doctrine of *transubstantiation.* The followers of the misnamed reformation all unite in denouncing this doctrine, as one of the greatest corruptions of the Catholic church; and in protesting against it as most irrational and unscriptural. Let us *try,* however, by the same rule as before, whether such protest be, or be not, well founded.

Once more, then, dear reader, imagine yourself to be standing, with your Catholic neighbor, before the judgment seat of Jesus Christ; and there called upon by him to *justify* your protest against this important doctrine, by producing in its support *sound* and *sufficient* reasons — such as may abide the scrutiny of Him who will then search into the very *secrets* and *intents* of your neart,[1] and whose word declares that he will judge according to *truth*.[2]

CHAPTER IV.

ON TRANSUBSTANTIATION.

JUDGE *to the Protesting Christian.* — "Before the feast of the Passover, when I knew that mine hour was come, that I should depart out of the world unto the Father, having loved mine own who were in the world, I loved them unto the end."[3] And this I manifested by instituting, at that time, the great sacrament of my love, wherein *I gave mine own body and blood for the life of the world.* For, "I took bread, and blessed, and brake, and gave to them, saying, *Take, eat* — THIS IS MY BODY. And I took the cup, and gave thanks, and gave it to them, saying, *Drink ye all of it* — *for* THIS IS MY BLOOD *of the new testament, which is shed for many for the remission of sins.*"[4] And all this was according to what I had before *promised* to give, when I said: "I am the living bread which came down from heaven: if any man eat of this bread, he shall live for ever: and the bread, that I will give, IS MY FLESH, which I will give for the life of the world."[5] Seeing, then, that *I* said, It "IS my flesh — This IS my body — This IS my blood;" why hast thou protested, saying, "It is NOT?"

A PROTEST AGAINST TRANSUBSTANTIATION, WHEREIN AN APPEAL IS MADE TO REASON AND THE SENSES.

PROTESTING CHRISTIAN. — Lord, all things are, indeed, in thy power — I have always believed that "with

[1] Rom. ii, 16; Heb. iv, 12, 13; Jer. xvii, 9, 10. [2] Rom. ii, 2. [3] John xiii, 1. [4] Matt. xxvi, 26, 27, 28; Mark xiv, 22, 23, 24; Luke xxii, 19, 20; 1 Cor. xi, 23, 24, 25. [5] John vi, 51.

God nothing is impossible;"[1] and therefore I dare not question thy divine Omnipotence. But yet I never could bring myself to believe, that it COULD be thy real body and blood which was given to thy apostles at the last supper; and therefore have I protested against the doctrine as absurd — as quite *contradictory to reason.* And all those who did believe it to be *verily* and *indeed* thy body and blood, I have always looked upon as *weak* and *credulous* — as men so far lost to common sense, that they would believe any thing that might be told them, no matter how *strange* or *absurd* it might be.

Indeed, how could I believe it to be thy body and blood, when *my senses* told me plainly enough, that it was only bread and wine? This and other absurdities, in the doctrine of transubstantiation, convinced me that it could *not* be so. I was obliged, therefore, to turn thy words from their plain and literal meaning, to a figurative and mystical sense; and herein the Holy Scriptures afforded me great assistance.

BOTH THE PROTEST AND APPEAL REBUKED AND REJECTED.

JUDGE. —"My wrath is kindled against thee, for thou hast not spoken of me the thing that is right:"[2] wherefore, "out of thine own mouth will I judge thee, thou wicked servant."[3] For, as the unbelieving Jews "spake against those things which were spoken by Paul, contradicting and blaspheming;"[4] *so thou* hast raised thy voice even against the things spoken by ME, contradicting and blaspheming the very words of the Lord thy God! Why hast thou not feared to prescribe limits to mine *almighty power?* Why hast thou dared to *measure it* by the *short* rule of human understanding? In all this thou art *without* excuse — thou hast *no cloak* for thy sin;[5] since it was written : "The things which are

[1] Luke i, 37; Matt. xix, 26. [2] Job xlii, 7. [3] Luke xix, 22. [4] Acts xiii, 45. [5] John xv, 22; Rom. i, 20.

impossible with men, are possible with God; . . . . for with God ALL *things* are possible."[1] But thou wouldst not believe my word.

PROTESTING CHRISTIAN.—Lord, this I have read, and have *believed*.

JUDGE.—This thou hast read and *professed* to believe, but it was a mere *empty* profession. For, as the unbelieving Jews, when they heard me say, "The bread that I will *give* IS MY FLESH, . . . strove amongst themselves, saying, *How can* this man give us *his flesh* to eat ?"[2] so thou, in like manner, hast protested against these same words of mine, as absurd and impossible. *I*, the ALMIGHTY, said, It "IS *my flesh*"—"*This* IS *my body*;"[3] but thou hast said, "It is NOT so—it CANNOT be—the words MUST be figurative." And thus, in order to explain away my words, thou hast presumed even to set bounds to mine Omnipotence!

Was not, then, the same power that changed water into wine at Cana, in Galilee;[4] and water into *blood* in Egypt;[5]—that converted the *lifeless* rod of Aaron into a *living* serpent, having both FLESH and BLOOD;[6] was not that same almighty power able also to change bread and wine into my body and blood? *Could not* I have so changed them, *if such had been my* WILL? and were not my positive and repeated declarations[7] a sufficient testimony that such *was* my will? Wilt thou dare to tell *me*, that if I had had the WILL to do this, I had not the POWER? And yet thou hast said this, in the very reasons whereby thou hast endeavored to support thy protest; all the while *professing* to believe that "with me all things were possible, . . . and nothing impossible."[8]

But, thinking to justify thy unbelief, thou has appealed from *my word* to *thy senses*, as bearing evidence, that, notwithstanding my plain and positive declara-

[1] Luke xviii, 27; Mark x, 27; Jer. xxxii, 27; Job xxxvii, 23, 5. [2] John vi, 52, 53. [3] Matt. xxvi, 26. [4] John ii, 1, 9, 11. [5] Exod. vii, 19, 20, 21. [6] Exod. vii, 9, 10, 12. [7] John vi, 51, 53, 54, 55, 56, see also note 4, page 41. [8] Mark x, 27; Luke i, 37.

tions, the bread and wine remained still *unchanged*.
How COULD they, thou hast said, be changed into my
body and blood, when *thy senses* told thee they were
still bread and wine? or, in other words, how could that
sacrament have all the appearances of being *bread and
wine*, and yet not be bread and wine, but body and
blood? how could it have the *appearances* of one thing,
and the *substance* of another? Thy senses, then, seemed
to bear evidence that it was bread and wine; my word
— my repeated declaration — bore evidence that it was
my body and blood: WHICH *was the greater testimony?*
When the Holy Ghost was seen descending upon me,
"in a BODILY SHAPE like a dove;"[1] and when, afterwards, the same Holy Spirit descended upon each of my
apostles, under the appearance of " cloven tongues, like
as of fire;"[2] why didst thou not raise there the same
objection, seeing there was the self-same difficulty? For,
hadst thou been present on those two occasions, thy
senses would have testified, that there were the *appearances of a dove* on one occasion, and of *cloven tongues*
on the other; and so far their testimony would have
been true, for there *were* those appearances.   But if,
from such testimony of appearances, thou hadst con-
cluded, that there was *therefore* the reality or *substance*
of a dove and of cloven tongues, thy *mistaken reason*
would have drawn a FALSE conclusion, opposed to the
declaration of the plain words of Scripture: for *no* dove,
no cloven tongues were there; but the Holy Ghost under
those appearances. *Just so* it was concerning the sacrament of my love: Thy senses testified, that there
were the *appearances* of bread and wine; and herein
their testimony was true, for there *were* those appearances.   From this testimony of appearances, thou con-
cludedst that there was *therefore* the reality or *substance*
of bread and wine; but herein thy *mistaken reason*
drew a FALSE conclusion, contrary to the repeated declaration of my plain words.

AN APPEAL TO THE SCRIPTURES IN SUPPORT OF THIS PROTEST.

PROTESTING CHRISTIAN.— Lord, I dare not say that thou COULDST NOT, by thy word, have made this change, and have given me thy body and blood under the appearances of bread and wine, *if such had been thy* WILL — *if such had been the* REAL MEANING *of thy words*: But I have protested against taking thy words in their literal sense, because the Holy Scriptures gave them a figurative and mystical meaning. And of such figurative explanation, they supplied me with many apt illustrations :

For, if thy words were to be taken figuratively, when thou saidst, "*I am the door*"[1] — "*I am the vine*,"[2] why not also, when thou saidst, "*This is my body?*"[3] Again, when thy apostle of the gentiles said, "They drank of that spiritual Rock that followed them, and *that Rock was Christ*,"[4] he meant to say, it was a *figure* of Christ.

THIS APPEAL ALSO REBUKED AND REJECTED.

JUDGE.— One of my apostles was inspired to foretell that there would come a time when men *would not* ENDURE *sound doctrine*, but *would turn away their ears from the truth*."[5] This thou hast done, and much more: for thou hast even *protested against the truth* and called it *falsehood!* and, in order to give to thy protest the *appearance* of truth, thou hast *perverted* my words, by *wresting them* from their natural and obvious meaning; following herein the example of those perverse and faithless Christians, who, in the days of my apostles, "would pervert the Gospel" that had been preached to them,[6] and wrested the written Word of Life unto their own destruction.[7]

[1] John x, 7, 9. [2] John xv, 1, 5. [3] Matthew xxvi, 26, 28. [4] 1 Cor. x, 4. [5] 2 Tim. iv. 3, 4; Luke xviii, 8; Heb. iii, 12, 18, 19. [6] Gal. i, 7. [7] 2 Pet. iii, 16.

Because I spoke *sometimes* figuratively, could that authorize thee to explain ALL my words in a figurative sense? or, to explain them figuratively or literally *at pleasure*, without regard to the context? When my beloved disciple recorded these words of mine — "I am the door,"[1] he expressly showed that they were the mere explanation of a "parable" which I had just been delivering to the Jews, saying, "Verily, verily, I say unto you, He that entereth not *by the door* into the sheepfold, but climbeth up some other way, the same is a thief and a robber: but he that entereth in *by the door*, is the shepherd of the sheep. . . This *parable* spake Jesus unto them : but they understood not what things they were which he spake unto them. Then said Jesus unto them again, Verily, verily I say unto you, I am the door of the sheep. All that ever came before me, are thieves and robbers."[2] But, when I said, "This is my body,"[3] there was *no* parable there, to show that my words were figurative.

Again, those other words, "I am the vine,"[4] to which thou hast appealed, were evidently the mere *application of a comparison*, which I had just made, saying, "Abide in me, and I in you. *As the branch* cannot bear fruit of itself, except it abide *in the vine:* NO MORE can *ye* except ye abide *in me.*"[5] So far the comparison. I then proceeded to apply it, saying, "I am *the vine*, ye are *the branches :* he that abideth in me, and I in him, the same bringeth forth much fruit: for without me ye can do nothing. If a man abide not *in me,* he is cast forth AS *a branch.*"[6] But, when I said, "*This is my body,*" there was no such *comparison there* that could give to my words a figurative meaning.

The words of my apostle, to which thou hast also appealed, prove nothing in thy favor, but rather do they stand against thee. For, when he said, "And the Rock was Christ,"[7] he was evidently not speaking of the ma-

[1] John x, 7, 9. [2] John x, 1, 2, 6, 7, 8. [3] Matt. xxvi, 26, 28. [4] John xv, 1, 5. [5] John xv, 4. [6] John xv, 5, 6. [7] 1 Cor. x, 4.

terial rock, but of what was prefigured by it; that is to
say, he was speaking of *me,* whom he called the *"spiritual Rock."* And were not his words to be taken in their
literal` sense? for, was not I that *"spiritual* Rock"
whereof the *material* rock was a figure? Could this,
then, authorize thee to wrest the words which I spoke
concerning *my body and blood* from their literal and
plain meaning to a figurative sense, contrary to the repeated explanation of them, which I myself had given?

A FURTHER APPEAL TO SCRIPTURE TO SUPPORT THE PROTEST.

PROTESTING CHRISTIAN. — Lord, in thine own words
on this very subject, I found some few expressions, by
means of which I turned all the rest to a figurative and
spiritual sense. For, after thou hadst declared to the
Jews, that " the bread that thou wouldst give, was thy
flesh, which thou wouldst give for the life of the world,"[1]
thou saidst unto them: " It is the spirit that quickeneth; the flesh profiteth nothing: the words that I speak
unto you, they are spirit, and they are life."[2] The
same explanation thou didst also give at the last supper.
For, after having said to thy apostles, " Take, eat; this
is my body which is given for you," thou didst immediately show the meaning of these words, by adding:
" This do in remembrance of me."[3] Hence, therefore,
ALL thy words on this subject I have explained in such
way as to make them mean, that I was to receive thy
body and blood — *not really and in deed* — but *by faith;*
that I was to receive bread and wine *in reality,* but that
I was to take it *" In remembrance of thee."*

THE APPEAL CONVICTS THE APPELLANT OF UNBELIEF.

JUDGE. — Thou wicked, thou faithless servant! "thou
hast perverted the words of the living God,"[4]— thou

[1] John vi, 51. [2] John vi, 63. [3] Luke xxii, 19; 1 Cor. xi, 24,
25. [4] Jer. xxiii, 36; Jer. v, 12; Gal. i, 7.

hast wrested them to thine own destruction.[1] For thou hast taken up *my words* to plead therewith the cause of thine *unbelief;* and they — the very same — testify against thee.

When, addressing the faithless Jews, I had declared to them, saying, "The bread that I will give, is *my flesh,* which I will give for the life of the world,"[2] they, like thee, would not believe my words; but "strove amongst themselves," as unbelievers have always done, "saying, How can this man give us *his flesh* to eat!"[3] Did I hereupon inform them that it was not MY FLESH that I meant to give, but only a figure of my flesh! or did I *confirm* what I had just before stated? Thou shalt hear my words: and, whilst thou hearest, tremble for thine unbelief? In words the plainest and simplest that language could furnish, and in declarations most positive and explicit, I answered and said:

"Verily, verily I say unto you, Except ye eat THE FLESH OF THE SON OF MAN, and drink HIS BLOOD, ye have no life in you.

"Whoso eateth MY FLESH, and drinketh MY BLOOD, hath eternal life, and I will raise him up at the last day.

"For *my flesh is meat* INDEED, and *my blood is drink* INDEED.

"He that eateth MY FLESH, and drinketh MY BLOOD, dwelleth in me, and I in him.

"As the living Father hath sent me, and I live by the Father: so, he that *eateth me,* even he shall live by me."[4]

After hearing these *plain* and *positive* and *repeated* declarations, the Jews could no longer doubt the meaning of my words; but, like thee, they would not believe them. Many of my disciples also, seeing that I really meant to give them *my flesh indeed to eat* and *my blood indeed to drink,* murmured in like manner at my words, and said, "This is a *hard* saying; who *can* hear it?"[5] Knowing in myself that they thus murmured at it, I

[1] 2 Pet. iii. 16. [2] John vi, 51. [3] John vi, 52. [4] John vi, 53, 54, 55, 56, 57. [5] John vi, 60.

reproached them for their *unbelief*, saying, "Doth this offend you? *What* and if ye shall see the Son of Man ascend up *where he was before?*"[1] that is to say, If you are offended at my words, because I said, I will give you *my flesh* to eat, and *my blood* to drink — if you find it *hard* to believe that I can do this, now that I am here *on earth* with you; how will you believe that I can do it, when you shall have seen me *ascend up into heaven?* Now, this I said, foreseeing that there would come a time wherein men, "not knowing the power of God,"[2] would make this very objection, and would say: — "Christ is *in heaven*, where he sitteth at the right hand of the Father; how then can he be also *on earth* in the sacrament?" Having thus added to their difficulty, instead of explaining it away, I then showed *them*, and now show *thee*, the cause of such *unbelief*, saying to them, "It is the spirit that quickeneth; the *flesh* profiteth nothing:° the words that I speak unto you, they are spirit, and they are life. But there are some of you that believe not. Therefore said I unto you, that no man can come unto me, except it were given unto him of my Father."[3]

Thus, then, because it was not "given them of my Father to come unto me," they believed not my words, but murmured at them as "a hard saying."[3] For, to

---

[1] John vi, 60, 61, 62. [2] Matt. xxii, 29. [3] John vi, 63, 64, 65.
[4] John vi, 60.

---

* Observe, Christ does not say, *my flesh*, but "*the flesh* profiteth nothing." He is not here speaking of *his own flesh* as profiting nothing; for *his flesh* profits us *much*, since it is *by its means* that we were redeemed. But he is speaking, in this passage, of corrupt human reason when unassisted by the Spirit of God. For wherever, in the New Testament, "the flesh" and "the spirit" are thus put in opposition to each other, by "the flesh" is invariably meant *the fleshly wisdom or corrupt reason of man*, and by "the spirit" is meant *reason enlightened and assisted by divine grace.* See Matt. xxvi, 41; and xvi, 16, 17; John iii, 6; Rom. viii, 1 to 14; Gal. v, 16 to 25; 1 Cor. ii, 5; 10, 12 to 15; 2 Cor. i, 12.

the believing of "the words of eternal life," the *carnal
mind* of man, or mere wisdom of the *flesh*, is of no avail;
because the *flesh* leadeth not to a belief of my words,
but to *unbelief:* "The works of the flesh are ... *heresies.*"[1] For the purposes of *faith*, therefore, "the *flesh*
profiteth nothing:"[2] for *faith* comes not from "the carnal mind," or "fleshly wisdom" of man; but is given
by the spirit:[3] "The fruit of the spirit is .... *faith.*"[4]
Wherefore, to arrive at faith, it is necessary to be drawn
by the Father[5]— to be "led by the Spirit of God;"[6]
because "it is the *spirit* that quickeneth"— that ani-
mateth the soul to a faith in my words: herein "the
flesh profiting nothing." This same truth I also taught
on another occasion, when, after Peter had professed a
firm faith in me, I said to him, "Blessed art thou, Simon
Bar-jona: for *flesh and blood*, (man's fleshly wisdom)
hath not revealed it unto thee, but *my Father* which is
in heaven."[7] Now, as the words which I had spoken
to the Jews, were *spirit and life;*[8⁰] to wit, were truths
proceeding from the *Spirit of God* and appertaining to

---

[1] Gal. v, 19, 20. [2] John vi, 63. [3] 1 Cor. xii, 9. [4] Gal. v, 22;
Eph. v, 9. [5] John vi, 44, 65. [6] Rom. viii, 14. [7] Matt. xvi,
16, 17. [8] John vi, 63.

* If it be contended that these words are an explanation of
those preceding passages wherein Christ promises to give us
his flesh to eat and his blood to drink, then how truly are his
words "spirit and life," according to the literal sense in which
the Catholic Church understands those promises? Christ not
only says, "He that eateth *my flesh* and drinketh *my blood*,"
&c., but "He that eateth *me*," &c. (verses 56, 57.) Wherefore, Catholics believe that *with the body and blood* of Christ,
which they receive in the holy Communion, *his soul and Di-
vinity* are inseparably united—they believe that they receive
his body *in that spiritualized and living state* as it was after his
resurrection. (1 Cor. xv, 42, 44; Rom. vi, 9.) How truly,
then, are his words "*spirit and life*," according to the Catholic
faith! But, according to the belief (or rather unbelief) of protesting Christians, his words are *neither* spirit *nor* life. For
they believe what they receive in the Communion to be truly
bread and wine — things *without* "*spirit*," *without* "*life*" —*lifeless* bread, *lifeless* wine.

eternal life, the Jews could not believe them, because they were not moved and *quickened* thereto by the *spirit,* as Peter was;[1] but were guided by the *flesh* or " *carnal mind* which *is enmity against God.*"[2] From this cause it was that *they* "went back and *walked no more with me.*"[3] And from the same cause also, in aftertimes, didst *thou* in like manner, and thy protesting brethren with thee, murmur at those same words of mine as " a hard saying," impossible to be believed, going away and *walking no more with my church — that faithful church,* which, after the example of Peter, believed my words, and taught them, knowing them to be " the words of eternal life."[4]

But, striving still to justify thyself in having thus imitated the unbelieving Jews, thou hast appealed to a few words spoken by me at the last supper, as giving to all the rest a figurative meaning. For, having said to my apostles, "Take, eat; this is my body which is given for you," I immediately added: " Do this in remembrance of me."[5] Now, *do what?* Evidently *that* which had just been done; to wit, *Eat my body* and *drink my blood* in remembrance of me, — when you eat my body and drink my blood, remember me — bear in mind that *that same body* which you eat was *broken for you* on the cross, and *that same blood* which you drink *was there shed for the remission of your sins.* And, verily, could I have left to mankind a memorial of my death more perfect or more striking than this? or could I have left them a surer pledge of my tenderness and love?[6] But, instead of acknowledging this my loving kindness towards thee, and repaying it with a grateful return, what hast thou done? Thou hast disbelieved my words, and protested against them; — scornfully rejected this pledge of my love, and supplied its place with an *empty shadow!* That what I gave to my apos-

---

[1] John vi, 68, 69; Matt. xvi, 16, 17. [2] Rom. viii, 7; 1 Cor. ii, 14. [3] John vi, 66. [4] John vi, 68. [5] Luke xxii, 19; 1 Cor. xi, 24, 25. [6] John xiii. 1.

tles tho night before I suffered, was *my very body and blood,* is a truth which *my words* had most explicitly declared, and of which *the Scriptures* gave the clearest and most positive testimony;[1] and yet, notwithstanding such evidence, thou hast protested against this doctrine, and esteemed it folly to believe it; — thou hast even uttered against it words of contumely and reproach, reviling it, contradicting it, blaspheming it; — thou hast kept at a distance from the church which I had commissioned to teach it; accounting thyself to be more wise in rejecting it, than was my church in believing it. But now, to thy sorrow, dost thou find, that thy wisdom in rejecting it, like that of the unbelieving Jews, was but the *wisdom of the flesh* — that earthly wisdom which is *foolishness* with God;[2] and that the folly of my church in believing my words, was *that folly* of which it was written: "God hath chosen *the foolish* things of the world, to confound *the wise;* . . . . that *no flesh* should glory in his presence."[3]

JUDGE *to the Catholic.* — And hast *thou,* also, disbelieved my words and protested against them? Hast *thou* also imitated those faithless disciples, who, upon hearing my words, said, "*This is a hard saying; who can hear it?*"[4] and so "*went back and walked no more with me?*"[5] Hast *thou* "fallen after the same example of unbelief?"[6]

THE CATHOLIC BELIEVES CHRIST UPON HIS WORD.

CATHOLIC. — Lord, to whom was I to go in search of truth, if I found it not in thee? "Thou hadst the words of eternal life."[7] And infinite thanks to the divine Goodness, that I was not left to follow the blind guidance of *the flesh,* and so to perish in *unbelief;* but that it was given me of the Father to come unto thee,[8]

[1] Matt. xxvi, 26, 27, 28; Mark xiv, 22, 23, 24; Luke xxii, 19, 20; 1 Cor. xi, 23, 24, 25; Luke i, 37; Matt. xix, 26; John vi, 53, 54, 55, 56, 57. [2] 1 Cor. iii, 18, 19. [3] 1 Cor. i, 27, 28, 29. [4] John vi, 60. [5] John vi, 66. [6] Heb. iv, 11. [7] John vi, 68. [8] John vi, 65, 44.

— that He quickened me by *the spirit* to believe **every** word that had proceeded out of thy mouth.[1]

For, *upon thy word* I have believed, that the bread which thou promisedst to give, was *thy flesh*, which thou didst give for the life of the world.[2] I heard, indeed, many around me murmuring at this, and saying with the Jews, "How can it be *his flesh*" — "How can this man give us *his flesh* to eat?"[3] But I imitated them not. Nothing could be more obvious than *the sense* in which thy words were to be taken; as to the meaning of them I could have no doubt whatever: since the very possibility of any reasonable doubt was utterly destroyed by those solemn and repeated declarations whereby thou didst so plainly and so positively *confirm* the words which the unbelieving Jews had objected to. Indeed, how could I doubt thy meaning, when I heard thee making, in answer to their objection, these clear and explicit and solemn protestations: "Verily, verily I say unto you, Except ye *eat the flesh* of the Son of Man, and *drink his blood*, ye have no life in you: — Whoso eateth *my flesh*, and drinketh *my blood*, hath eternal life, and I will raise him up at the last day; — For *my flesh is meat indeed*, and *my blood is drink indeed;* — He that eateth *my flesh*, and drinketh *my blood*, dwelleth in me, and I in him; — As the living Father hath sent me, and I live by the Father: so, he that *eateth me*, even he shall live by me?"[4] It was evident from the objection of the Jews, that THEY had taken thy words literally, as meaning thy very flesh: "How can this man give us *his flesh* to eat?"[5] When, therefore, I heard thee (who camest not to deceive, but to instruct) so emphatically *confirming* them in that literal sense, I could not but see that *that sense* was the one intended: and, accordingly, *upon thy word* I have believed, that if I would "dwell in thee, and thou in me" — if I would "have life in me, and be raised up at the last day to eternal

[1] Matt. iv, 4. [2] John vi, 51. [3] John vi, 52. [4] John vi, 53 to 57. [5] John vi, 52.

life," I was, for these purposes, to eat THY *flesh* and
drink THY *blood:* for upon thy word I have believed,
that THY *flesh* was meat (not in figure,) but *indeed*, and
THY *blood* was drink *indeed.* Far, therefore, have I
been from disbelieving thy words; far have I been from
going away from thee in unbelief, as did those unhappy
disciples, who, murmuring at thy words, exclaimed, —
" This is a hard saying; who can hear it?"[1]   But, on
the contrary, I have followed the example of St. Peter,
who, however *hard* thy words may have appeared to
the flesh or *man's carnal wisdom*, was quickened by *the
spirit* to yield to them nevertheless his firm assent — to
believe with a sure faith, that, hard or not hard, they
must be true, — that they must be " the words of eternal
life," because they were the words of " the Son of the
living God."[2]

And, moreover, when I found thee, the night before
thy passion, taking bread into thy sacred hands, and
blessing, and breaking, and giving to thy apostles, saying, " *Take, eat;* THIS IS MY BODY:" and like manner
taking the chalice also, and giving it to them, saying,
" *Drink ye all of it, for* THIS IS MY BLOOD *of the New
Testament, which is shed for many for the remission of
sins;*"[3] I could not but see that this was the literal fulfilment of those former words wherein thou hadst *promised* to give us THY FLESH to eat, and THY BLOOD to
drink.[4]   And, as it was not for me to contradict or gainsay thy positive declarations, *upon thy word* I have believed, that what thou gavest to thy apostles on this
solemn occasion, *was thy very body and thy very blood,*
— that it was *the body* GIVEN *for them and the blood*
SHED *for them* — according to the express declaration of
thy divine Word.

And in these words of thy apostle to the Corinthians:
" The cup of blessing which we bless, *is it not the com-*

---

[1] John vi, 60. [2] John vi, 68, 69. [3] Matt. xxvi, 26, 27, 28;
Mark xiv, 22, 23, 24; Luke xxii, 19, 20; 1 Cor. xi, 23, 24, 25.
[4] John vi, 51 to 57.

munion of the BLOOD *of Christ?* The bread which we break, *is it not the communion of the* BODY *of Christ?*"[1] in these words I had the unspeakable satisfaction to see, that, in having thus *believed* thee upon thy word, I had imitated the faith of that great apostle. For, in those words, I found him believing, that in these divine mysteries, there really was *a communion of thy body and blood,* — that thy sacred *body and blood* were herein *communicated* to the receiver. And more especially did I see that *this was his belief,* when I found him, immediately after, not merely teaching the same doctrine in the plainest words, but, moreover, drawing from it such conclusions, as rendered all reasonable doubt of his meaning impossible. For, after he had related to the Corinthians the sacred words of institution, namely, " I have received of the Lord that which also I delivered unto you, That the Lord Jesus, the same night in which he was betrayed, took bread; and when he had given thanks, he brake, and said, Take, eat; THIS IS MY BODY *which is broken for you :* this do in remembrance of me. After the same manner also he took the cup, when he had supped, saying, *This cup is the New Testament* IN MY BLOOD : this do ye, as oft as ye drink it, in remembrance of me ;"[2] after he had related these sacred words of institution, he proceeded immediately to *reason* upon them after this manner : " For as often as ye eat this bread,° and drink this cup, YE DO SHOW THE LORD'S

---

[1] 1 Cor. x, 16.　[2] 1 Cor. xi, 23, 24, 25.

° Because, in some passages, the Scriptures speak of the Holy Communion under the name of "this bread," Protesting Christians eagerly catch up the expression to form therefrom an objection against the Catholic doctrine. But their objection has no *real foundation.*

For, *if* we must conclude that *no change* has taken place in the bread and wine, because the Scriptures, when speaking of the sacrament, sometimes says, "this bread;" then we must in like manner conclude, that when "Aaron cast down his rod before Pharoah, ... and *it became a serpent,*" and when the magicians also "cast down every man his rod, and *they became*

DEATH till he come."' Nothing, indeed, could more
strikingly and more vividly "show thy death," than
this manducation of thy real body and blood. For even
the *mere act* of individuals eating the body and drinking
the blood of a victim—eating the very body that was
"*broken* for them," and drinking the very blood "*shed*
for them"—the mere act of doing this necessarily *showed the death* of that victim. As often, therefore, as this
was done by thy faithful, they did necessarily and lite-

' 1 Cor. xi, 26.

serpents," (Exod. vii, 10, 11, 12,) *no change* had here taken
place, because *after this* the Scripture still calls them *rods:*
"But Aaron's *rod* swallowed up their *rods*." (Exod. vii, 12.)
We must conclude also, that when Moses had changed all the
waters of Egypt into blood, *no such change* had taken place,
because the Scripture still calls it *water:* "And all the waters
that were in the river, *were turned to blood* . . . . and the river
stank; and the Egyptians could not drink *the water* of the
river." (Exod. vii, 20, 21.) And when Christ had changed
water into wine at the marriage feast of Cana, we must here
again conclude that *no such change* had taken place, because
the Scripture still calls it *water:* "When the ruler of the feast
had tasted *the water* that was made wine, and knew not whence
it was, but the servants which drew *the water* knew," &c. (John
ii, 9.) In like manner also, when Christ had opened the eyes
of the man *born blind,* (John ix. 6, 7,) we must conclude that
the man *had not received his sight,* because, after his eyes had
been opened, the Scripture still calls him "the *blind man*."
(John ix, 17.)

Now, will Protesting Christians say, that these various
changes had *not* taken place, merely because what had been
declared *serpents,* are again called *rods*—because what had
been declared *blood,* and *wine,* are again called *water*—and because he whose eyes had been declared *opened,* is again called
the blind man! If they will not say this, then *why* do they say
that no change had taken place in what Christ gave to his
apostles at the last supper, merely because what He then declared to be *his body,* is sometimes again called *bread!* It is
evident from the examples just given, that when one thing has
been changed into another, it is the usual language of Scripture
to call it still by the name of what it *was before* the change had
taken place. Evidently, then, the objection has no *real* foundation.

rally "show THY death." But, by eating something else as a *substitute* for a body, or as a *figure* of it — this would not *show* whether that body *was slain* or *not* — it would not, and could not, *show its death*. How clearly, then, does the reasoning contained in these words of thy apostle, prove that he had believed thee upon thy word — that, like me, *he* had believed in the manducation of thy real body and blood. And still more forcibly in his words that immediately followed, did he show that such *was* his belief; " Wherefore, he said, whosoever shall eat this bread, or drink this cup of the Lord unworthily, shall be guilty of the BODY AND BLOOD of the Lord. . . . For he that eateth and drinketh unworthily, eateth and drinketh *damnation to himself, not discerning the Lord's body.*"[1] Manifestly, then, this apostle did himself believe, and taught the Corinthians also to believe, that thy most sacred body — not mere symbols or figures of it, but thy most sacred body itself — was *outraged* by the unworthy receiver. He believed, therefore, that thy body was *present* in the sacrament; otherwise, the Communicant, by receiving unworthily, could not have been *guilty of it;* for, *had it not been there*, he could not have interfered with it at all : neither could he, in such case, have brought upon himself the terrible sentence of *damnation* for *not discerning* THY BODY in the sacrament; since he *could not* have discerned it *there*, where it was not.

Thus, then, in having *believed thee upon thy word*, I had the unspeakable comfort and satisfaction to see that herein I was following the faith and example of this great apostle, who declared that he had received his faith by a special revelation from thyself.[2] For my faith then on this subject, resting as it does on such sure grounds, I can have no fear of condemnation. Indeed, so *plain*, so *positive* were thy words, that I could not and dared not have believed otherwise than I have done. Again,

[1] 1 Corinthians xi, 27, 29. [2] 1 Corinthians xi, 23; Galatians i, 11, 12; Eph. iii, 3.

therefore, calling heaven and earth to witness,[1] with the most perfect confidence do I now declare, that if in my belief on this subject I have been deceived, Lord, it is thy very own words that have deceived me: for, as *thou hast said*, so precisely I have *believed*.

JUDGE *to the Catholic.*— Blessed art thou, because thou hast not been offended in my words[2] — because thou hast not followed the unbelieving Jews, in going away from me or my church *in unbelief;*[3] but hast had it given to thee of my Father to come unto me — hast been quickened by the Spirit to imitate the faith of my apostle, in believing my words implicitly, as being "the words of eternal life."[4]

REFLECTIONS ON CHAPTER IV.

Here, dear reader, let me again call your attention to a few reflections:

The Catholic church teaches, from the express words of our blessed Redeemer, that in the holy communion we receive — not mere bread and wine — but the VERY BODY *and* BLOOD *of Christ.* Now, against this doctrine you have protested: and yet, have you not just seen that this doctrine rests on the very words of HIM in whom you profess to believe? Reflect, therefore, I entreat you — reflect seriously upon the awful nature of your protest. Ask yourself the following very important questions:

"When I protest against this doctrine of the Catholic church, am I not thereby protesting against the very word of God — against the plainest words and most positive declarations of my Redeemer? For, when He says, 'The bread that I will give is MY flesh;'[5] do I say with Him and with the Catholic, 'It is so?' Do I not, on the contrary, protest and say, 'It is *not* so?' When He says, 'Except ye eat *the flesh* of the Son of Man,

---

[1] Deut. iv, 26. [2] Luke vii, 23; John vi, 61. [3] John vi, 52, 60, 66. [4] John vi, 67, 68, 69. [5] John vi, 51.

and drink *his blood*, ye have no life in you;"[1] do I say
with Him and with the Catholic, ' It is *his flesh* and *his
blood* that I must receive?' Do I not, on the contrary,
protest again and say, ' It is *not* his flesh and blood that
I am to receive, but only bread and wine — mere symbols of his flesh and blood?' When He says, ' My flesh
is meat INDEED, and my blood *is drink* INDEED;"[2] do I
say with Him and with the Catholic, ' It is so INDEED?'
On the contrary, do I not still protest and say, ' His
flesh and blood *are not meat* INDEED, but IN FIGURE
only?' Again, when He says, ' This IS MY BODY *which
is given for you* — This IS MY BLOOD *which is shed for
the remission of your sins;*[3] do I say with Him and
with the Catholic, ' It IS his body, that same which was
given for me — It IS his blood, the same which was
shed for me?' On the contrary, do I not here again
protest and say, ' It *is not* that body — It *is not* that
blood?' It is true, my Redeemer says ' it *is;*' and I say
' it *is not:*' He says ' it is *his body;*' I say ' it is only a
figure or *symbol* of his body.' "

Ask yourself, dear reader, such questions as these —
and give them your serious attention. For, to *disbelieve*
and *protest against* the very words of Christ himself, as
you do when you protest against this doctrine, is a matter of most serious consequence; since Christ positively
declares, " He that *believeth not* shall be damned;"[4] and
his apostle likewise says, that " without *faith* (which is
the evidence of things not seen) it is *impossible* to please
God."[5] How awful therefore, are the consequences of
unbelief — of *protesting against* the truths delivered by
our Redeemer! It is to warn you against drawing upon
yourself these dreadful consequences, that this same
apostle admonishes you against falling into the *unbelief*
of the Jews: " Take heed, he says, lest there be in any
of you *an evil heart of* UNBELIEF, in departing from the

[1] John vi, 53. [2] John vi, 55. [3] Matt. xxvi, 26, 27, 28; Mark
xiv, 22, 23, 24; Luke xxii, 19, 20; 1 Cor. xi, 23, 24, 25. [4] Mark
xvi, 16. [5] Heb. xi, 1, 6.

living God;"[1] and to show the importance of attending
to this admonition, he asks the following question: "To
whom sware He that they should not enter into his rest,
but to them that BELIEVED NOT? So we see that they
could not enter in BECAUSE OF UNBELIEF."[2]

Seeing, then, that *unbelief is a crime* which debarred
the unbelieving Jews from entering into God's rest; will
not the same *crime of unbelief* debar you also from entering in, if it should be found that you, like them, are
guilty of it? and have you not reason to reproach yourself with *unbelief*, if you gainsay the very words of your
Redeemer — if you protest against his plain and positive
declarations? and *do you not* gainsay his very words —
his plain and positive declarations, *when you deny the
reality of his body and blood in the sacrament?* Oh!
then, dear reader, reflect seriously upon the *awful circum-
stances* in which your protest places you: and rest not
satisfied with *reflecting only*, but be determined moreover,
that, in spite of any obstacles, you will *act* according to
the *real dictates* of truth and conscience. Bear in mind,
that Religion is a subject whereon depends your happiness, or your misery, FOR ETERNITY!

THE CONCLUSION.

THE consequences, then, of *protesting against truths revealed by God* being of so very serious a nature, beware,
I entreat you, how you protest against *this doctrine;* and
not against *this only*, but against *the other doctrines also*
of the Catholic Church. For you have seen, that those
doctrines of the Catholic Church, which have been ex-
amined in the preceding pages, and against which you
have been taught to protest, are doctrines in exact
accordance with the Holy Scriptures—that they are
contained in the very words of God himself; and, conse-

[1] Heb. iii, 10, 11, 12. [2] Heb. iii, 18, 19.

quently, that your protest against them is a protest, not merely against the teaching of *the Catholic Church*, but also against the very teaching of *God*.

How *unjust*, therefore, towards your Catholic breth ren, and how highly *criminal*[*] before God, must such a protest be! Is it then to be persevered in? Are you not, on the contrary, bound in conscience to *cease from it?* and not to cease from it *merely*, but are you not obliged, moreover, in the sight of God, to BELIEVE AND EMBRACE THOSE VERY TRUTHS OF HIS, AGAINST WHICH YOU HAVE HITHERTO PROTESTED; seeing they are truths which he himself has so clearly revealed?

OBSTACLES TO CONVERSION PUT IN THEIR PROPER LIGHT.

I am fully aware indeed, that, at the very idea of ta king such a step as the one here shown to be obligatory, a thousand difficulties will present themselves to your mind. For, however strongly you may feel convinced *of the truth* of Catholic doctrines, and consequently, *of the obligation* of professing them; early prejudices and worldly connexions will, nevertheless, forcibly incline you to adhere still to your former opinion:

"*What!* (you will say) *can I leave the religion where in I was* BORN — *the religion I have been* BROUGHT UP TO *from a child?*" This question will be best answered by another: When the Jews, refusing to embrace the true doctrines of Christ, continued still in the religion where in they had been brought up, did their having been brought up in the Jewish religion excuse them before God for continuing in it, after the truth had been made

---

[*] When I say "*criminal before God*," I mean to except the case of *invincible ignorance.* To whom this exception may ap ply God knows; but certainly *not* to those who wilfully shut their eyes against the truth, — *not* to those who will not either hear or read, but *avoid information*, *lest* they should be con vinced of the truth, and should feel themselves obliged in con science to embrace it.

known to them? Most certainly *not*. Then can the like reason excuse you?—The only question should be, Is the religion wherein you have been brought up, *the true one or not?* If *not*, then *must* not *it* be rejected and *the true one* embraced?

" *But* (you will add) *can I forsake the religion of my parents — of my relatives and friends, to embrace the one which their souls abhor, and which they will esteem it weakness and folly in me to believe? Can I take such a step as this, foreseeing, as I do, that it will excite their displeasure, and perhaps set them against me during the remainder of my days?*"— Here again the only question should be, Is the religion of your relatives or friends *the true one* or *not?* If *not*, then you *must* renounce *it* to embrace *the truth.* And if, by so doing, you displease them, set them against you, or cause them to reproach you, or persecute you, or cast you off, painful as these things may be to human nature, you *must* nevertheless obey the voice of truth and conscience—you must "obey *God*, rather than *men.*"[1] For, on this point, the words of our Redeemer are most positive and decisive: "Think not, he says, that I am come to send peace on earth...For I am come to set a man at variance against his father, and the daughter against her mother" (*to wit*, by requiring them to follow the truth in spite of the violent opposition they will meet with from kindred and friends)......"And a man's *foes* (i. e. *obstacles* to his following the truth) shall be they of his own household. He that loveth father or mother more than me, is not worthy of me: he that loveth son or daughter more than me, is not worthy of me."[2] "If any man come to me, and hate not his father, and mother, and wife, and children, and brethren, and sisters, yea, and his own life also, he cannot be my disciple;"[3] *that is to say,* If you are not ready, for the sake of following the truth, to renounce any thing in this world, *however near*

Acts v, 29. [2]Matt. x, 33 to 37. [3]Luke xiv, 26 Matt xix. 29.

or dear it may be to you, you cannot be Christ's disciple—you are not worthy of him. If your friends, then, make opposition to your embracing the *true* religion of Christ, you have to choose between two things: whether you will *renounce the truth* for the sake of the friendship of this world; or, *renounce the friendship of this world* for the sake of obeying the truth.

"But (you will say) a still further difficulty presents itself: for, were I to embrace the Catholic religion, I should incur the displeasure, not only of my relatives and acquaintances, but of those persons also on whom *I depend* for my situation in life or for success in my business: I fear I should be removed from my present situation, or lose my means of support." These, like the former, are only *human* considerations, in answer to which, the words of our Redeemer are equally *positive* and *decisive*: For he says, "Whosoever he be of you, that forsaketh not *all* that he hath, he cannot be my disciple:"[1] *that is,* Whoever is not willing to suffer *any earthly loss, rather* than be prevented from *obeying the truth,* cannot be Christ's disciple; and hence the divine word elsewhere declares, That they who *do not obey the truth,* so far from being acknowledged at the last day as his disciples, will be treated by him with *indignation and wrath.*[2] But, on the other hand, such as resolved to obey the voice of truth and conscience, in spite of any difficulties or any earthly considerations whatsoever, — *such as these* are his disciples indeed, and *to such* he has made promises most encouraging and consoling: "Verily, verily I say unto you, There is no man that hath left house, or brethren . . . or lands *for my sake and the Gospel's,* but he shall receive a hundred fold *now in this time; . . . .* and *in the world to come* eternal life;"[3] by which words our Lord reminds us, that God *can and will* abundantly recompense us for whatever loss we may suffer for the sake of him and his revealed truths. For, indeed, *are not* ALL THINGS *in the hands of his Providence?* cannot

[1] Luke xiv, 33. [2] Rom. ii, 8. [3] Mark x, 29, 30.

God make you either fail or prosper, just as he pleases;
and is not a faithful compliance with his will the surest
way to incline him to make you prosper? Be determined, therefore, FIRST OF ALL to do what God requires of
you — to obey the voice of truth and conscience; and
then, as to any temporal disadvantages that may threaten you for so doing, you need not fear, but resign yourself, in this respect, entirely into the hands of his Providence: " *Cast thy burden upon the Lord, and he will
sustain thee:*"[1] "Take no thought, saying, What shall
we eat, or what shall we drink, or wherewithal shall we
be clothed. . . . For your heavenly Father knoweth that
ye have need of all these things. But *seek ye* FIRST *the
kingdom of God and his righteousness*, and ALL THESE
THINGS SHALL BE ADDED UNTO YOU."[2] Now, will you
mistrust these positive promises of Christ? have you no
dependence on his word? for does He *promise*, and *not
fulfil?* Let but your *first* solicitude be, to obey his will
resolutely from your heart—to obey the truth;—let
there be nothing wanting on your part to the fulfilment
of his promises; and then, like David, confidently may
you say, "Though I should walk through the valley of
the shadow of death, I will fear no evil;"[3] for, " *In God*
have I put my trust: I will not be afraid what *man can*
do unto me."[4] And, moreover, for your consolation
and greater encourgement, raise up your eyes to heaven,
and behold there the eternal recompense *promised . to
those that suffer for conscience sake;* for, under all such
sufferings, Christ says to you : " *Rejoice and be exceeding
glad; for great is your reward in heaven.*"[5]

---

[1] Psalm lv, 22. [2] Matthew vi, 24 to 34; Luke xii, 22 to 31.
[3] Psalm xxiii, 4. [4] Psalm lvi, 11. [5] Matt. v, 10, 11, 12; 1 Pet.
iii, 14.